SHEIKH'S
PRINCESS OF
CONVENIENCE

SHEIKH'S PRINCESS OF CONVENIENCE

DANI COLLINS

MILLS & BOON

First published in Great Britain 2018
by Mills & Boon, an imprint of HarperCollins*Publishers*
1 London Bridge Street, London, SE1 9GF

Large Print edition 2018

© 2018 Harlequin Books S.A.

Special thanks and acknowledgement are given to
Dani Collins for her contribution to the
Bound to the Desert King series.

ISBN: 978-0-263-08195-4

MIX
Paper from
responsible sources
FSC
www.fsc.org FSC® C007454

Printed and bound in Great Britain
by CPI Group (UK) Ltd, Croydon, CR0 4YY

To my fellow authors, without whom
the romance genre wouldn't exist.
You have given me hope and tears and
guidance and passion, and best of all a belief
in happily-ever-after. Also a special shout out
to my fellow authors in this quartet—
Tara Pammi, Maya Blake and Caitlin Crews.
I'm privileged to have met each of you in
person and you are all wonderful in every way.

CHAPTER ONE

DO I LOOK PRETTY, Mama?

The reflexive question, one she had learned to suppress, still jammed in Galila's throat along with her heart when she turned and caught sight of an apparition.

She held herself motionless on the tiled platform in the center of the reflecting pool, staring at the woman who appeared against the window to her mother's lounge. With the subtle golden glow cast by the lights around the courtyard, it seemed as though her mother looked out at her, watchful and unsmiling.

As usual.

Galila wore a stunning tangerine gown, strapless and with a skirt of abundant shimmering silk. A long-sleeved tulle overlay was embroidered and bedecked with silver and glittering

jewels—as suited a member of the royal family
on the new king's wedding day. Her hair cas-
caded from beneath a tiara that only ever came
out on special occasions, and until now, only on
her mother's head.

The dress was too young for her mother, but
those were definitely her mother's eyes, scrupulously emphasized with greens and gold, liquid
eyeliner ending in a cat's tail. At one time, those
doe-like eyes would have swept over Galila with
indulgence. Affection.

So pretty, my pet. Her painted lips would have
smiled with tender love as she stroked Galila's
hair.

Tonight, Galila's mouth—as sensuously curved
as her mother's had been and wearing her mother's signature glossy red—tightened. Her ele-
gantly arched brows drew themselves together as
she critically sought flaws, exactly as her mother
would have done if she had still been alive.

Your skin looks sallow, Galila.

It was the yellow light and her imagination, but
the reproach still had the power to sting. To make

her yearn to correct the flaw and recapture the love that had dried up and blown away like sand across the desert.

She ought to be glad her mother wasn't here; ought to be grieving properly for a life lost. Instead, it was her secret shame that she was mostly grieving her chance to win back her mother's love. Or perhaps just to understand how she'd lost it.

What had she done that was so terrible— except to grow up looking exactly as beautiful as her mother had been? Was that her great crime?

Could she finally bloom freely now that she wouldn't overshadow her mother?

She lifted the glass she held, leaving another kiss print on the rim.

Not champagne, either, Mother. She directed that baleful thought to her image and received a dispassionate glance in return.

The brandy she had learned to drink at boarding school seared with blessed heat through her arteries, promising the numbing effect Galila sought.

In a perfect world, she would drink herself unconscious and possibly drown here in an inch of water, escaping the chaos raging around her.

Don't make a spectacle of yourself, Galila. That's Malak's purview.

"Your dress is getting wet."

The male voice, so deep and velvety it matched the caress of the warm night air, had her turning to peer into the shadows, expecting—well, she didn't know who she expected. A man, yes, but not *such* a man.

He leaned against the edge of an archway, features sharpened by the low light and framed by the drape of his *ghutra*. He was dangerous and handsome at once. Dangerously handsome with those dark, deeply set eyes and strong jaw beneath a short, black beard. Breath-stealing, in fact, in his gold-trimmed *bisht* that might have been the color of a good merlot. It hung open across wide shoulders to reveal his embroidered *thobe*, tailored to his muscled chest, collar closed at his throat and decorated by a yellow sapphire the size of her fist.

She told herself it was the alcohol that made her sway, but she suspected it was the impact of his virility.

He straightened and held out a hand. "Come. Before you ruin perfection."

He sounded indifferent, perhaps a little impatient, but her confused, bruised-up heart reached like a flower toward the sunshine of his compliment. She used her free hand to lift her skirt and carefully placed her feet on each round tile. She was a little too drunk for stepping stones and appreciated when he took the drink from her hand and clasped her forearm, balancing her until she was completely away from the water.

His touch undermined her equilibrium as much as the brandy, though. More, perhaps. Brandy didn't make her chest feel tight and her eyes dampen with longing. Her ears picked up the distant sound of the wedding music, but all her senses were trained on him. Something in her flowed toward him. Sought...*something*.

He was tall, radiating magnetism while a force field seemed to surround him, one that made him seem untouchable. It cracked fissures through her that she couldn't begin to understand.

Maybe it was the brandy causing this overwhelming reaction.

He smelled the glass and his mouth curled with disdain. He set the glass aside.

"You don't approve of alcohol?"

"I don't approve of drunkenness."

It should have sounded too uptight for words, but she was ever so sensitive to censure. His condemnation cut surprisingly deep. Why? He was nothing to her.

But he was also like nothing she'd ever experienced—and she'd seen a lot these last few years, living in Europe. He wasn't like any of the urbane aristocrats or earnest artists she'd met. He didn't even match what she expected here, in her home country of Khalia. He was almost too iconic in his arrogant sheikh demeanor. She had long decided that if she ever did marry, it would be to a progressive, cultured man from abroad. Not one of these throwback barbarians from five centuries ago.

Yet he was utterly fascinating. A tendril of desire to impress him wormed through her. She wanted to stand here and hold his attention and earn his regard.

Quit being so needy, she heard Malak say in her head. He had learned to live without love or anyone's good opinion. Why did she think it was necessary?

She didn't, she told herself and reached for the glass. "It's my brother's special day. I'm celebrating."

"People do stupid things when they're drunk." Sheikh Karim of Zyria didn't raise his hand or his voice. He didn't even tell her not to drink.

Nevertheless, his deep tone carried the quiet command instilled by his station. It was evidently enough to make her falter and reassess him, perhaps understanding she would ignore him at her own peril.

He returned her scrutiny, taking advantage of the chance to do so up close. That's what he told himself he was doing, in any case.

He had watched the royal family all day and evening—the ones who were here, at least. Princess Galila, with her stark resemblance to her deceased mother, fascinated him the most. She flitted like a bird from perch to perch, joining this group and that, welcomed by all and animated as she spoke, flirtatious and not above rolling her eyes at anyone, including her brother, the groom and newly crowned King of Khalia.

Had her mother possessed that same sparkling energy? Was that how she had so ensnared his father? He had seen photos of all of them over the years, but in person, Princess Galila was not merely beautiful. She was potent and enthralling, pulling at him in a way he resisted out of principle.

Out of self-preservation, a voice whispered deep in the back of his mind.

Not that he was in danger of infatuation, he assured himself. She struck him as far too superficial, thriving on being the center of attention. The way she smiled and bantered told him she was fully aware of the power in her beauty and sex appeal. She used it without shame to steal the spotlight from every other woman in the room.

That's why it had surprised him when she'd slipped into the garden and walked away from the party into the family's private courtyard. He had followed because he wanted to understand how this woman's mother had destroyed and re-shaped his entire life, not because he had been compelled to keep her in his sights.

Had her mother, Queen Namani, been this vain? He'd watched Galila preen in front of her own reflection like a lovebird, so deeply enam-ored with herself that she hadn't been aware of his presence.

He wasn't a stalker, lurking in shadows, spy-ing on pretty maidens. He was a king, one with questions he had never been able to answer. Be-sides, he wanted to see her up close. Discover the secret of her allure.

He'd called her out of the pool—which was when he'd realized she was drunk.

Disappointing. He abstained, never wanting to

be so far into his cups that he thought a leap off a balcony would solve his problems.

When he'd told her drinking was unwise, he'd thought for a moment that despair clouded her eyes, but she'd quickly switched to using her stunning looks to distract and mesmerize.

"What's stupid about enjoying myself?" she challenged lightly. She lifted her hair off her neck and let it flow carelessly off her forearm, watching to see if he followed the movement.

There was a man inside this royal casing. He felt desire the same as any other, but he knew when he was being invited to lose focus by ogling a breast. Much as he longed to eye the weight of her curves, he kept his gaze locked with hers.

"Exhibit A. You're on a tear of self-destruction." Locking horns with him was a grave mistake, he silently warned.

She was disconcerted by his unaffected response. She might even have been burned by it. Her brow flinched. She quickly lifted her chin in a rally of spirit, though.

"Perhaps I have reason. Did you think of that?" Her long lashes blinked in big, innocent sweeps.

"I'm sure your life is very fraught," he said drily.

"I lost my mother three months ago," she threw back at him with quiet anguish. "I'm entitled to grieve."

"You are." He dipped his head, but that was as much condolence as he was willing to offer. He hadn't been allowed any self-pity after his father's death. The circumstances had been far more disturbing and he'd been a child of six. "Drinking yourself blind will only make things worse."

"How is *that* possible?" she cried softly. "My father is so grief-stricken, he's like a shell. I can't reach him. No one can." She looked to the huge window where her own reflection had stood. "He misses my mother terribly."

Karim understood that affliction, too. No matter what he did, he had never been able to ease his mother's heartbreak over her loss, either. Protecting her from the fact that his father's death had been a suicide was the best he'd ever been able to do.

"She had an affair," Galila whispered. "He loved her anyway, but now we all know about it, which seems to have tripled his agony."

Karim's heart stopped. Even the breath in his lungs stilled.

As if she noted his jolt of alarm, she nodded to confirm her shocking statement, eyes wide and tortured.

"Your father knew but kept it from you?" Karim's mind raced. He had never confided in a single soul, no matter how long and heavily the truth had weighed on him—and it had. Endlessly. With the death of Queen Namani, he had thought that at least the secret of the affair would die when he did.

"He's known for years!" Her tone rang with outraged astonishment. "He helped her cover it up when she became pregnant. They sent away our half brother the day he was *born*."

Karim had to concentrate on keeping his face expressionless, his feet rooted to the marble tiles so he didn't fall over. His ears rang as though the soft words had been a cannon next to his head.

Galila gave a choking half laugh of near hysteria. "Explain to me how one processes *that* sort of news except to get roaring drunk?"

"You have a third brother? A half brother?" *He* had a half brother? His carefully balanced world wasn't just tilting on its axis. It was reaching such a sharp angle everything was sliding into a jumbled mess at his feet.

"Yes!" She didn't seem to notice his deep shock, too caught up in layers of emotional turmoil within herself. "My brothers and I should have been supporting each other, comforting our father, but *he* showed up at the funeral. Told us how our mother had been writing to him for *years*. How she regretted sending him away because she *loved him best*." Her eyes gleamed with a thick sheen of tears. "Because he was her only link to the man she truly loved."

Her fist went to the spot over her breast where she seemed to stem the cracks in a bleeding heart.

"Our father had a complete breakdown. Who

wouldn't? We nearly all did! Zufar had to step in and take over… And now that's where Zufar's intended bride is, with *our half brother*." She spoke with livid bewilderment, arm flinging out to some unknown location. "Zufar wasn't supposed to marry Niesha. Amira's been promised to him since she was born, but Adir came back this morning and talked Amira into running away with him. I watched her go through the window. Adir said it was his revenge for being denied his birthright."

"Adir," Karim repeated faintly. That was the name of his brother? He barely heard the rest of what poured out of her.

"Zufar is so single-minded, he married our *maid* rather than admit there was anything wrong. Malak has quit the palace entirely, gone gambling or to work his way through a harem, I imagine. Where does that leave me? With *no one*. So excuse me if I take some comfort in a bottle of brandy."

When she started to drink, he stole it and tipped

the alcohol onto the tiles. He had to. This news was utterly explosive.

"Who else have you told?" he demanded.

"No one," she muttered, giving a *tsk* of annoyance at the brandy puddle. "Now I have to walk all the way back for a fresh one."

"Who is Adir's father?" He kept his voice level but held the empty glass in such a tight grip he expected it to shatter in his hand, leaving him dripping blood onto the evaporating alcohol.

"No one knows." She gave her hair a flip. "Mother took *one* secret to her grave, it seems. Although, I have half a mind to ask around that crowd." She jerked her chin toward the balcony across the darkened expanse of the garden, where light poured out the open doors to the palace ballroom. "He must be there."

The elite from all the neighboring kingdoms mingled in a kaleidoscope of colored gowns and robes. Voices competed with the music in a din that suddenly grated on him more than he could bear.

"Why do you think that?" he asked, forcing a

tone of mild curiosity while his blood prickled in his veins.

"My mother wouldn't take up with a servant. It had to have been someone of her stature, very likely one of those men congratulating my brother on his mismatched marriage."

She was right, of course. His father had been exactly at her mother's level, not that Karim would confirm it. Maybe the affair had started at an event like this, he imagined. His father and her mother would have been about his and Galila's age when they met, in their prime and bursting with biological readiness. Perhaps they had slipped away into the shadows to indulge their passion, as other couples were doing even now.

He was far too practical to wish, but he had an uncharacteristic longing to be one of those carefree couples with Galila. If only he could enjoy a simple dalliance, like other people, rather than listening to her sing his personal scandal to the night sky while racking his brain on how to most quickly prevent it going further than his own ears.

She was inordinately desirable, he noted with determined detachment. He almost understood his father's desolation at being rejected by such a woman. Of course, his father had been married and never should have started the affair in the first place, but Karim had no such restrictions.

In fact, remaining close to this pretty bird was exactly what he ought to do. He had devoted his life to ensuring his mother never learned the truth about his father's death. He wasn't about to watch it all come apart through one woman's brandy-lubricated tongue. In fact, he had to ensure the entire family's silence on the matter.

Hmm.

"We should get back to the party," the mysterious stranger said.

Through her haze of growing infatuation, Galila distantly realized she shouldn't be loitering alone with a man, let alone spilling family secrets in his ear, but there was something exhilarating about holding his attention. For weeks, in many ways *years*, she'd been an afterthought.

Female, and therefore less than her male brothers. Princess, not queen.

"Mmm, yes, I'd love to fetch a fresh brandy," she said with a cheeky slant of her lashes at him.

No smile of answering flirtation, only a circumspect look that made her heart sink under the feeling she had disappointed him.

"I don't need your permission," she pointed out, but her confidence was a stuttering thing in her chest.

"We'll see," he said cryptically and took her arm to steer her around the pool.

His touch sent a shock of electricity through her. She jolted and nearly turned her ankle. It was disconcerting, made even worse by his disapproving frown.

I'm not that drunk, she wanted to claim, but all coherent thoughts seemed to have left her brain.

Her entire being was realigning its magnetic poles with something in him. She wasn't just aware of him. His presence beside her seemed to surround her in a glow that tingled her skin and warmed her blood. It compressed her breaths while making her feel each one come into her like scent, except it was his aura she was taking into herself.

In a daze, she let him guide her toward the path that would lead them into the garden and back to the wedding reception.

"You don't drink at all?" she asked, trying desperately to ground herself in reality.

"Never."

"Oh, please," she teased, leaning into his firm grip on her elbow. "Let me be the one to initiate you."

Some dim instinct for self-preservation warned her that provoking him was a terrible idea. Something deeper, even. A sense that her gentle mockery not only failed to impact him but was misplaced. He wasn't weak at any level. Nor innocent. He was worldly to the point of cynical, and inimitably strong because he allowed no one to influence him.

Looking up at him as they entered the garden, she noted that his mouth was a work of art. Despite how very serious it was, his lips were full and sensual. How would they feel, crushed against hers?

The flush that went through her at that thought was pure lust, hitting in all her erogenous zones and making her feet tangle into themselves again.

He stopped and steadied her, frowning. "Do I have to carry you?"

She laughed at the thought of it. She was worldly enough to have fooled around with men, but she knew who she was. She had kept her reputation intact along with her virginity for the sake of her family. Maybe even to avoid one more harsh criticism from her mother. The deep-down truth, however, was that she'd never been overcome with enough desire to give her body to anyone.

The compulsion to throw herself into the arms of this man, tonight, was intense enough to unnerve her. A drunk and stupid idea, indeed, but exciting. She didn't even know his name!

"What were you doing over here? Following me?"

"Same as you." A muscle in his cheek ticked. "Reflecting."

"On?"

"Responsibility."

"How boring. I'm surprised I didn't find *you* drunk and facedown in that pool."

The severity in his expression didn't ease. His hold on her arm sent glittering sensations through her bloodstream. She ought to shake him off. What would people think if they returned together? Nothing good, that was certain.

Such a remarkable man, though. One she really didn't want to share with a party full of beautiful women. She wanted him to be hers. To look on her with adoration and desire.

His expression in the moonlight was cool and decidedly intent. Ruthless, even. But there was hunger buried deep beneath his layers of control. Avid male need that she had seen often enough to recognize it. His narrowed eyes focused on her mouth, telling her his speculation was along the same lines as her own.

"Don't you want to throw caution to the wind sometimes? I do." She flipped her hair behind her shoulder again. *Look at me. Want me.* "Malak gets away with it all the time. I'm tired of being the good girl."

"Are you?" Something in his silky tone and the way he flicked his gaze down her front wound around her like ribbons, exciting and wicked. Tightening and binding, compressing her breaths, yet making her feel free.

"Am I tired? Or a good girl? I'm both." She thought of her charity work, her carefully culti-vated image of kindness and purity, her endless striving to earn her mother's approval and her stalwart presence beside the men in her life as they took their own self-destructive paths.

All her life, she had tried to be like her mother. They had all thought Queen Namani so perfect, but she hadn't been. Why should Galila live up to something that was an illusion? Live up to the expectations of a woman who not only hadn't held herself to such high standards after all but was also *dead*.

"I'm ready to do what I want." She pressed her-self to his front and lifted her mouth.

"I don't take advantage of inebriated women,"

he said, but with a glance toward the light of the party. His cheeks hollowed, giving his profile a chillingly ruthless appearance. His hands on her arms tightened in some internal struggle.

"I'm not that drunk," she dismissed in a sultry voice. She was low on inhibition, certainly, but more intoxicated by the excitement he made her feel.

They were in a faraway, unlit corner of the garden, where the scent of roses and herbs, orange blossom and frangipani coated the air, making it feel thick as a blanket around her.

"Kiss me," she demanded when he hesitated.

His hands almost began to push her away, but he only held her like that, staring into her uplifted face. For three heartbeats that shook the entire world, they stood like that, as he debated and came to a decision.

With a muttered imprecation, he circled his arms around her. His fingers dove into her hair, tilting back her head as his mouth came down to cover hers.

For another pulse of time, that was all it was.

One mouth against another while the universe seemed to open itself, leaving her utterly vulnerable yet transfixed by the vast beauty of it.

With a harsh noise in his throat, he dragged his lips across hers. Instantly they were engulfed in a kiss that was beyond anything she had ever experienced. Intimate and passionate. Hot and damp and demanding. A statement of possession but with a quality that swept her into abandoning herself willingly. Joyfully.

The texture of his tongue met her own, boldly erotic. She reacted with a moan and mashed herself into him so hard her breasts hurt, but it felt good, too. The contact assuaged the tips that stung like bites. When he started to ease back, she whimpered and pressed her hand to the cloth covering his head, urging him to continue kissing her with this mad passion. She wanted to feel his hair, taste his skin, strip naked and know the weight of him over her.

She wanted to know how that hard flesh that was pressing against her belly would feel stroking inside her.

With an abrupt move and a ragged hiss of in-drawn air, he pulled back. "Not here."

Had he read her mind? Her body?

"My room," she whispered, already plotting their discreet path through the halls of the palace.

"Mine," he stated. She couldn't tell if it was a preference of location or if he was staking a claim on her. Either way, she let him take her hand and drag her from the garden toward the stairs that led up to the balcony outside the ballroom.

She balked in the shadows at the bottom of the steps. "My lipstick. People will know."

"I thought you were ready to take control of your own life?"

In the slant of light, she saw a mercilessness curl at the corner of his mouth. He pivoted them a few steps into the shadows beside the wall of the steps.

She was more than ready to give herself to him, but this was her home. Her brother's wedding. She was the Princess of Khalia. She was sober enough to know that she had to be discreet about having an affair, not parade it through the middle of a state ceremony.

But as her would-be lover pressed her to the stones that had barely cooled in the hours since sundown, she forgot her misgivings. Her hands found the heat of his neck and she parted her lips, moaning as he kissed her again.

He transported her to that place of magic they seemed to create between them.

As she lost herself to his kiss again, he stroked her hip and thigh, urging her to pick up her knee and make space for him between her legs. Cool air grazed her skin as he shifted her skirt up, up and out of the way, touching—

She gasped at the first contact of fingertips against the back of her thigh. Arrows of pleasure shot into her core, making her yearn so badly her eyes grew damp along with her underthings. She arched her neck as he trailed his mouth down her throat.

It was exquisite and joyful and…

Wait.

He was hard where he pressed between her legs, but something was off.

She touched the side of his face, urging him to lift his head. There was heat in his glittering eyes, but it was banked behind a cooler emotion. Something deliberate. His skin might have been flushed with arousal, but his expression was dispassionate.

He wasn't as involved as she was.

Hurt and unease began to worm through her, but before she could fully react, she heard a gasp and a giggle above them. Someone said a pithy, "Get a room."

"That's the princess!" a female voice hissed.

"With who?" She knew that demanding masculine voice. She looked up to see several faces peering down at them over the wall of the balcony, one of them her brother's. He did *not* look pleased.

Did her lover release her leg to find a modicum of decorum? Not right away. Not before she caught a dark look of satisfaction in his hard features.

Gaze solely on her, he very slowly eased his hold on her leg so his touch branded into her skin as she lowered her thigh. Humiliation pulsed in her throat, made all the more painful by the way he had gone from passionately excited to…this. Remote. Unaffected. Perhaps even satisfied by her public set down.

Angry and embarrassed as she was, her abdomen still tightened in sensual loss as he drew away from their full-frontal contact, which only added to her mortification.

"You were right," he said. "We should have gone to your room."

She had no choice but to take refuge there. Alone and *fast*.

CHAPTER TWO

GALILA WOKE TO a dull headache, some low-level nausea that was more chagrin than hangover and a demand that she present herself to her brother *immediately*.

Despite what she would have hoped was a fulfilling wedding night, Zufar was in a foul mood and fifteen minutes in, didn't seem to be tiring of tearing strips off her.

"You can't bring that sort of shame down on the palace and think it doesn't matter."

"What shame?" she cried, finally allowed a word in edgewise. "A few people saw us kissing. Malak behaves far worse *all the time*."

"And you hate it when he gets the attention! You couldn't put your own silly need to be in the spotlight on hold for one night? The night of my wedding? Is anyone talking about our ceremony or my bride? No. The buzz is all about the fact you were seen behaving like a tart."

"You're welcome," she said with a glance at her manicure. "Because the things they were saying about your marriage to the maid weren't all that flattering."

"Mind how you talk to your king, little sister," he said in a tone that should have terrified, but she refused to take him seriously. It was just the two of them in here and he was behaving like a Neanderthal.

"I don't know what you want me to do," she said, throwing up her arms. "I can't undo it."

"You could start by promising you'll show more decorum in future. This shouldn't even be happening. Why Mother let you go this long without marrying you off to someone who can control you, I will never understand."

"Can't you?" she bit out sharply.

"What is that supposed to mean?"

"She saw me as competition, Zufar." It was plain as day.

"Get over yourself, Galila. *You* are the one who

sees everyone as competition. Take heed now. I won't have you upstaging my queen. You will learn to take a back seat."

"I wouldn't—"

They were interrupted by a servant. He entered after a brief but urgent knock and hurried to lean into Zufar's ear. All Galila caught was "...very insistent..."

Zufar's expression hardened. "Show him in." As she turned, Zufar added, "Where do you think you're going?" He glared at Galila's attempt to exit.

"I assumed we were done."

"You wish. No, I have no idea why he insists on speaking to me, but I imagine it concerns you, so you'll stand here while he does."

"Who?" She looked to the door the servant had left through.

"Sheikh Karim of Zyria."

"Is that his name?" She had imagined he was one of their more illustrious guests but hadn't realized—

Zufar slammed his hand onto his desktop, making her jump. "Do not tell me you didn't even know the name of the man who had his hand up your skirt."

She looked to the corner of the ceiling, biting the insides of her cheeks.

"Do you honestly think my life has room for your childish antics?" Zufar demanded.

She started to scowl at him, but *he* came in. Sheikh Karim of Zyria. He had exchanged his ceremonial garb of last night for a Western-style bespoke suit in slate gray sans headdress.

If possible, he was even more knee-weakeningly handsome. The crisp white of his shirt and blood-red tie suggested a man who commanded any world he occupied. He stole the breath from her body in a psychic punch, utterly overwhelming her.

His gaze spiked into hers as though he'd been waiting to see her again, but before her heart fully absorbed that sensation, he offered a terse nod and turned his attention to her brother, leaving her feeling promptly dismissed and inexplicably bereft.

* * *

After ensuring Princess Galila had indeed retired for the night, Karim had gone to his own guest apartment, somewhat disgusted with himself. He had been telling the truth when he'd claimed not to take advantage of women in a weakened state. He considered himself an honorable man.

But he hadn't been able to take the chances that she would leak his secret to someone else after her next sip of brandy.

He had been wrestling with his conscience over whether he should seduce this tipsy woman to his room, where he could at least contain her, when she had thrown herself against him in the darkest corner of the garden.

Their kiss had been the most potent drug imaginable, jamming into his veins and bringing him throbbingly alive at the first taste of her. As if he'd been dead for three decades. Existing, yet not seeing or tasting or smelling. Not *feeling*.

Then, for heart-stopping minutes, he had been resurrected. Sunlight had dawned upon him, shaking him awake from a long freeze. Everything in him had wanted to plunge into that world and never leave it.

Somehow, he had pulled back, much the way any sane man would catch himself before teetering like a crazed addict into a hallucinogenic abyss.

That shockingly intense reaction had been a lesson. One he would heed. Now he knew *exactly* how dangerous she was. It meant he was now prepared to withstand the power of her effect on him.

He kept telling himself his abominable actions were for honorable ends. He was protecting her family as much as his own. His deliberately public display had worked beautifully to put an end to any inquiries she might have made about the man who had impregnated her mother.

Temporarily.

The rest of his strategy would play out now.

With one brief glance, he took in her suitably demure dove-gray skirt and jacket with a flash of passion-pink blouse beneath. Her hair was rolled into a knot behind her head, but she was every

bit as beautiful as she'd been last night, if looking a little haunted around the eyes and pouty
around the mouth.

He didn't allow his gaze to linger, even though
the flush on her skin was a sensual reminder
of her reaction to him last night. She had worn
a similar color when their kisses had sent the
pulse in her neck racing against the stroke of his
tongue. That response of hers had been as beguil-
ing as the rest, and not something he could allow
himself to recollect or he'd embarrass himself.

For the most part, Karim kept his emotions behind a containment wall of indifference. It wasn't
usually so difficult. He'd been doing it his whole
life.

Last night, however, this woman had put more
than one fracture in his composure. Those tiny
cracks had to be sealed before they spread. His
reaction to her would be controlled. His command of this situation would be logical and deliberate. Effectual—as all his actions and decisions
were throughout his life.

He started by refusing to react with any degree

of emotion when her brother offered a blistering, opening attack.

"I expected better of a man in your position, Karim." Zufar didn't even rise, lifting only one sneering corner of his mouth. "You should have had the grace to be gone by now."

"Allow me to make reparation for any harm to your family's reputation," Karim said smoothly. "I'll marry her."

Galila gasped. "What? I'm not going to marry *you*."

Karim flicked a glance to her outraged expression. "Do not tell me you are promised elsewhere." He had to fight to control his reaction, never having experienced such a punch of possessiveness in his life. He would shed blood.

"No." She scowled. "But I'm not ready to marry anyone. Certainly not a stranger. Not just because I kissed you. It's ridiculous!"

"It's highly practical and a good match." He had spent much of the night reasoning that out, determined emotions wouldn't enter into this arrangement. "You'll see," he assured her. Her flair of passion could wait for the bedroom.

"I will not see!"

"Quiet." Zufar held up a hand, rising to his feet.

Galila rushed forward and brushed it down.

"Don't tell me to be quiet," she hissed. "I will decide whom I marry. And while it's a kind offer—" she said in a scathing tone that suggested she found Karim's proposal anything but, she stared Karim right in the eye as she said emphatically, *"No."*

Her crackling heat reached toward him, licking at the walls he forced himself to keep firmly in place.

"Clearly your sister has a mind of her own." She was the kind of handful he would normally avoid, but greater things were at risk than his preference for a drama-free existence. "Was that the problem with your first bride?" Karim asked Zufar with a blithe kick below the belt. "Is that why she ran off with your brother?"

"What?" Zufar's voice cracked like a whip,

but Karim kept his gaze on his intended bride, watching her flush of temper pale to horror.

"Half brother, I mean," he corrected himself very casually, despite feeling nothing of the sort. This was high-stakes gambling with a pair of twos he was bluffing into a straight flush.

"Galila." Zufar's tone was deadly enough that Karim shifted his attention—and the position of his body—to easily insert himself between the two if necessary.

Incensed as her brother looked, he didn't look violent. And culpable as Galila grew, she didn't look scared. She was glaring blame at Karim.

"Why are you doing this?" Her voice was tight and quiet.

"I am in need of a wife. Or so my government takes every opportunity to inform me." It wasn't a lie. "You are of suitable… What was the word you used when describing your mother's lover? Station? Stature. That was it."

"This goes beyond even your usual nonsense," Zufar said in a tone graveled with fury. "A moment ago, you didn't even know his name, yet you talked to him about our family's most intimate business?"

"I was drunk." She looked away, cheeks glowing with guilt and shame. "That's not an excuse, but it's been a very trying time, Zufar. You know it has. For all of us."

Zufar's eyes narrowed on her and his cheeks hollowed, almost as if he might accept that as reason enough for her imprudent behavior.

"Allow me to assure you," Karim said with scalpel like precision, "that if you agree to our marriage, your family's secrets will stay between us."

The siblings stood in thunderous astonishment for a few moments.

"And if I don't agree to the marriage?" Zufar asked, but Karim could see they both already knew the answer.

"Blackmail?" Galila asked with quiet outrage. "Why would you stoop so low? Why do you *have* to?" she challenged sharply.

He didn't. He hadn't made marriage a priority for a number of reasons, most of them superfi-

cial and convenience-related. He was a worka-
holic who barely had time for his mother, who
still very much needed him. Women expected
things. Displays of emotion. Intimacy that went
beyond the physical.

"I'm not going to hurt you, if that's what you're
suggesting," Karim scoffed. "I'll treat you as gently and carefully as the pretty little bird you are."

"In a gilded cage? You know, you could ask me
to marry you, not trap me into it."

"Will you marry me?"

"*No.* I would never have anything to do with
someone as calculating and ruthless as you are."

"You already know me so well, Princess, you're
practically made for me. It certainly seemed that
way last night."

Zufar made a noise of outrage while Galila
stomped her foot, blushing deep into her open
collar.

"Stop talking about that! There are other
women," Galila insisted. "Pick one."

"I want you."

"I won't do it."

Karim only swung his attention back toward her brother. "I've made it clear what I'm prepared to do to get her."

"Why? What else do you want?" Zufar flared his nostrils in fury.

Above all, Karim wanted to forestall any speculation about who might be the mysterious man their mother had fallen for. If it became known that Queen Namani's lover had been his father, King Jamil, the news would not only destroy his mother, but it would rock both kingdoms right down to their foundations. Not to mention what this newly discovered half brother might do with the knowledge.

So Karim only asked, "Is it so remarkable I might want her?"

"You didn't even introduce yourself. Last night was a setup," Zufar said.

"Oh, thank you very much," Galila interjected hotly, but hurt and accusation lingered behind her glossy eyes as she glared at Karim. "I don't care what you threaten. I'm not some camel you're trading."

Karim had given his explanation some thought as he had lain awake last night, having anticipated that Zufar would be a man of intelligence, capable of seeing his sister was being used for reasons that went beyond her obvious charms.

"I'm not the only man who noticed last night that the princess is very beautiful," he said to Zufar. "She's unmarried and much is changing in Khalia with you taking your father's place. An alliance with the sister of the new king could only be an advantage to me."

"And you think I want to form an alliance with a man of your methods?" Zufar scoffed.

"If I'm married to your sister, yes. I think we will both work toward aligning our countries' goals. And I believe, in the long run, you'll appreciate my methods. I'm saving you months of fielding offers from lesser men and having to play politics in refusing them."

"Such magnanimity," Zufar said with venom-like sarcasm, adding darkly, "But I can't refute the logic."

"Try harder, Zufar," Galila said scathingly. "Because I won't marry him and you can't make me."

"I'm your king, Galila." He said it flatly, but not unkindly.

As she tried to stare down her brother, her cross expression slowly faded into something disconcerted. She clearly began to realize what she was up against and grew pale.

"Zufar, you can't."

"I am not Mommy and Daddy whom you can manipulate with your crocodile tears. You have stepped way over the line this time. I can't put this back in the box for you."

It was tough love in action, something Karim would normally subscribe to, but he sensed genuine distress in the way she reached for a tone of reason, though her voice trembled.

"This isn't like our parents' time when everything was arranged and Mommy was promised to Daddy from when she was a girl. We are allowed to marry for love—"

"Did *I* get the bride I wanted?" Zufar interjected. "The time we are in, Galila, is one where we all have to make sacrifices for the crown of Khalia. You made this bed you're already half in." He sent a dark look at Karim. "Whether you were seduced into it or tricked or went there of your own volition."

Karim didn't bother explaining that as far as that side of it went, she had been a willing partner. He might not be a man who indulged his passions, but he and Galila certainly hadn't lacked any. That was the one thing that made him cautious about this arrangement, but that was a worry for a later time, after he got what he wanted.

Which was *her*.

Even though she looked shattered by his demand for her hand. She visibly shook but found the courage to turn and confront him. "I refuse. Do you understand me?"

"Come," Karim responded, holding out his hand, almost moved to pity by her anxiety but not enough to change his mind. "It is done."

"It is not," she insisted. "I'm going to talk to my father."

"You should inform him," Karim agreed. "Do that while I negotiate our marriage contract with your king."

Her father offered no help whatsoever. He gave her a halfhearted pat on her cheek, eyes red and weary.

"It's past time you married. Listen to your brother. He knows what is best for you."

No, he doesn't!

Malak didn't even answer her text. Her friend Amira was gone—seduced into running away with Adir. Galila was jealous of her friend. Amira's escape might have been dramatic, but at least she wasn't forced into a marriage she didn't want.

Galila felt as though she was being kidnapped in slow motion. Even her one trusted ally within the palace, Niesha, had gone from being someone who might cover for her long enough for a get-away to being her *queen*. Galila wasn't allowed to see her without an appointment and didn't have time to make one. A travel case had already been packed for her and Karim was knocking on the

door to her apartment while she flittered back
and forth in a panic.

"Ready?" The detached question made her long
to dismiss him as a robot, but there was something deeply alive about him. He was a lion—all-
powerful and predatory, completely unfeeling in
what he pursued or how much pain he caused,
so long as he could feast on whatever it was he
desired.

"I will never forgive you for this," she said in
reply.

"Let's save our vows for our wedding day."

"There won't be one." She used a glare that un-
failingly set a man in his place, but he was impervious, meeting her icy gaze without flinching.

Much to her chagrin, as she maintained the eye
contact, she felt the tug of desire all over again.
His eyes were such a dark brown they were almost black, velvety and holding far more depth
than she initially gave credit for.

The whole time he had been blackmailing her
brother and admitting that he had manipulated
her last night to capture her hand before anyone

else could, she had been thinking about how delicious he had made her feel.

She had thought about him *all* night, mostly feeling disappointed that they'd been caught and interrupted, not nearly as mortified as her brother had wanted her to feel when he had criticized her behavior.

But the enigmatic stranger who had kissed her was gone. He had turned into this disinterested man who had used her. His complete lack of reaction toward her, his utter indifference, reminded her that all the feelings and attraction had been on her side. That thought carved a hole right next to the ones already leaving a hollow feeling inside her.

Even if it was about time she married, even if she absolutely had to succumb to marriage, it should be to a man who wanted *her*. Not Zufar's sister. Not the Princess of Khalia. Not the politically expedient ally. *Her.*

He ought to at least offer her the adoration her mother had had from their father. No one should expect her to accept *this*.

And yet, as they walked outside to the cars, a polite round of applause went up.

For appearance's sake, her brother had announced that their engagement had been kept secret for weeks, so as not to overshadow the coming wedding. If Zufar thought the departing wedding guests believed that, there were several bridges in America he could purchase at an excellent price.

Repulsed as she was by the lie, she didn't make a scene. Far too late for that. She accepted congratulations with a warm, delighted smile. Let them all think this was as grand a romance as her brother tried to package it.

The better to humiliate Karim when she left him in the dust.

"Are you really a sheikh?"

Oh, had his fiancée finally chosen to speak to him? He glanced up from his productive hour on his laptop.

She hadn't cried or begged as they left the palace, which he had half expected. She had thrown waves of cold, silent resentment at him, making it clear that if he hadn't personally escorted her into the car and then his helicopter, she wouldn't be here.

As a man highly in demand and averse to theatrics, Karim told himself that receiving the silent treatment was a gift. At the same time, he had to acknowledge her strength of will was more than he had bargained for. He wasn't someone who thrived on challenge and overcoming conflict. He didn't shy away from it, either. He met obstacles head on and expected them to get out of his way.

This woman, however, with her royal blood seething with passion, wasn't cowed by the mere timbre of his voice. On the surface, she appeared soft and delicate, but he was beginning to see the length of steel in her spine.

He hoped like hell that didn't portend clashes. He had no time for tantrums.

"I am," he answered mildly.

Her skeptical gaze left the window to scan the interior of the helicopter cabin, then dropped to the clothes he'd changed into for travel. He'd worn a suit for his high-stakes meeting with her brother but wore typical Arab attire as often as possible. Not for religious or political reasons, but because he found it the most comfortable.

"I was not expecting company when I left Zyria," he explained of his helicopter and its lack of attendant. It only seated four in the cabin, but very comfortably. "This aircraft is the fastest and most flexible." He could fly it if he had to and regularly did, to keep up his skills. He would be doing so now, if she wasn't here, not that she seemed to want his company.

Her brows lifted in brief disdain as her attention went back out the window. Her frown increased and he almost smiled, realizing why she was skeptical.

The metropolis of his country's capital, Nabata, was not appearing beneath the descending helicopter. Instead, all she would see out there was a speck of a palace in the rugged desert.

"My mother is looking forward to meeting you. She spends much of her time at the palace my father built for her away from the city." She liked to escape grim memories.

It almost felt an insult to bring the daughter of his father's lover to meet his mother, the Queen Mother Tahirah. She had no idea of her husband's infidelity, of course. Keeping the knowledge from her was why Karim had orchestrated to marry Galila, but *he* knew. It grated against his conscience along with the rest of the secrets he kept.

Galila noted his expression and asked, "What?" with a small frown. She looked hurt as she touched the scarf she had tucked beneath her popped collar, then glanced down to ensure her skirt and jacket were straight. "Is my hair mussed?"

He cleared whatever shadows had invaded his expression. "No. You're beautiful. Perfect."

Her thick lashes swept down and she showed him her profile, but he knew she was eyeing him, suspicious of his compliment.

"You are and you know it," he chided. "Don't expect me to pander to your vanity."

Her painted mouth tightened. "Because I'm not a person whose feelings you care about or even an object you desire. I'm a rung on a ladder."

He pursed his lips, weighing her words and the scorn beneath them.

"Our marriage is expedient, yes. That doesn't mean it can't be successful. Many arranged marriages are."

"When both parties agree to said marriage, I'm sure they are."

They landed and disembarked, forestalling further debate—which was unproductive at this point. She was going to marry him and that was that.

"This is very beautiful," Galila said, gazing on the pink marble and intricately carved teak doors.

While Karim agreed, he found the extravagance of the palace disturbing. Clearly his father had been eager to please his wife with it. This wasn't a guilty conscience. He had built it before Queen Namani had come into the picture. Sadly, whatever he had felt for Karim's mother had been overshadowed by what he had felt for the other woman. And Karim and his mother hadn't been enough to live for, once Queen Namani ended their affair.

What, then, must his father have felt for Queen Namani if his first—and supposedly lesser—infatuation had produced this sort of monument? It was a depth of passion—of possession—Karim couldn't wrap his head around. He instinctively shied away from examining it too closely, maintaining a safe distance the way he would a conflagration or other life-threatening force.

As Galila started up the steps, he touched her arm, halting her.

She stilled and seemed to catch her breath. A soft blush rose under her skin.

Her reaction caused an echoing thrill inside him, one that warned him that he was tying himself to a ticking bomb and had to be very careful. On the surface, this physical compatibility might be exciting and promise a successful union, but he knew what indulged passion could do to a man.

He yanked the reins on his own response, hard,

especially as he realized he was taking advantage of every opportunity to touch her and still had his palm on her arm. He dropped his hand to his side with self-disgust.

She was looking right at him and whatever she read in his expression made a tiny flinch cross her features. It was gone so fast, he could have been mistaken, but it slid an invisible wall between them, one that niggled at him.

She lifted her chin to a haughty angle. "Yes?"

"You'll be kind to my mother."

Her spine grew tall with offense. "I'm always kind." She flipped her hair. "I was being kind last night when I let you kiss me."

It took him a full second to understand that the unfamiliar sensation in his throat was an urge to laugh. He couldn't recall the last time he'd loosened up enough for *that*, and fought it out of instinct.

At the same time, a deeper reaction—not ego, but definitely something that had roots in his masculinity—was affronted at her dismissal of their kisses last night. He knew exactly how potent they had been and didn't care for her trying to dismiss that inferno as "kindness."

The impulse to *show* her… But no. He refused to allow her to disarm him in any way. He waved her forward. "I'll look forward to your next act of kindness, then."

She narrowed her eyes.

"Come." He broke the eye contact. He could not, under any circumstances, become enamored with her. He had seen with his own eyes what falling for her mother had done to his father. He would not be another casualty to a Khalia temptress.

Despite its compact size and remote location, expense had not been spared on the desert palace. Galila was no stranger to wealth, but even she had to appreciate the effort of transporting marble and teak doors.

Inside, a fountain provided a musical ripple of noise and cooled the air. Columns rose three stories to a stained-glass dome. Mosaics in green and blue covered the walls to eye height before switching to delicate patterns in golds and blues and tangerines. Wrought iron marked the second- and third-floor walkways that encircled this grand foyer.

"I don't know what this is. A genie's lamp?" She was in love. "It's too beautiful for words."

Karim drew her up some stairs so thickly carpeted their shoes made no sound. They entered his mother's parlor where he introduced her to the Queen Mother Tahirah.

The older woman rose to greet them, her face holding deeply etched marks of grief that reminded Galila of the ones her father wore.

"It's like Queen Namani has come to visit me. Her beauty survives, if not my dear friend herself," she said, taking Galila's hands as she studied her features. "I'm so sorry for your loss."

"Thank you," Galila murmured, returning Tahirah's kisses against her cheeks, genuinely touched by her condolence. "I didn't realize you knew my mother, but of course you must have met her at some point through the years."

Was it her imagination that Karim stiffened? She glanced at him, but only saw the aloof expression she couldn't read. The one that stung because it felt like a condemnation for reasons she didn't understand.

"When we were young, yes," his mother said, drawing her attention back to her. "We often met up after we were both married, but lost touch after my husband passed. My fault. I ceased most of my royal duties and rarely went on social visits. I couldn't face the responsibilities without my soul, Jamil. Thankfully Karim's uncle was able to manage things until Karim was old enough to take his rightful position. And now my son has found happiness." Her faint smile was a weak ray of light in her otherwise anguished expression.

Oh, yes, they were both quite giddy and could hardly contain themselves, Galila thought, but she *was* kind to the less fortunate. Tahirah might be surrounded by extravagance, but she was the living embodiment of money not buying happiness. Her heart was clearly broken and had been for a long time.

"I expect we will both be very content as we go into the future," Galila prevaricated, adding a silent, *separately*. Read the news, gentlemen. Times had changed.

"And the wedding?" Tahirah asked.

"Within the month," Karim said firmly. "As soon as it can be arranged."

Galila stiffened, wondering if he had been planning to ask her about the timeline, but kept her pique to herself as Tahirah drew her across to the satin-covered loveseat.

"There's time for you to wear my engagement ring, then. I had it brought out of the safe."

"I...don't know what to say." Galila looked from the velvet box that Tahirah presented to her, then looked up to Karim, completely taken aback.

He nodded slightly, urging her to accept it.

She opened it and caught her breath.

An enormous pink diamond was surrounded by white baguettes. The wide band was scrolled with tendrils of smaller diamonds, making it as ostentatious as anything could be, but it was also such a work of art, it had to be admired. Coveted and adored, as every woman would want to be by her fiancé as she anticipated joining with him for a lifetime.

Her heart panged at the love that shone from such a piece, something she would never have if she married this man. She swallowed, searching for a steady voice.

"This is stunning. Obviously very special. I'm beyond honored." And filled with anguish that this was such a farce of a marriage when this ring was clearly from a marriage of total devotion. "Are you quite sure?" She looked again to Karim, helplessly in love with it but not wanting to accept something so precious when she was quite determined to abandon him at the first opportunity. She couldn't be kind *and* lie to this poor woman.

"I am." Tahirah said with a husk in her voice. "I haven't worn it in years, but it is beautiful, isn't it? Karim's father loved me so much. Spoiled me outrageously. Built me this palace…" She blinked nostalgia-laden eyes. "Losing him still feels as raw today." She squeezed Galila's hand. "And I'm quite sure Karim is as enamored with you. He has always told me he was waiting for the right woman. I'm delighted he finally found you."

Galila conjured a feeble smile that she hoped his mother interpreted as overwhelming gratitude. She felt very little conscience in defying her brother or even Karim, but misrepresenting herself to Tahirah was disrespectful and hurtful. She was genuinely sorry that she was going to disappoint her.

Karim took the ring from the box and held out his hand for Galila to offer hers.

His warm touch on her cool fingers made her draw in her navel and hold her breath, but it didn't stop the trickle of heat that wound through her, touching like fairy dust to secretive places, leaving glittering heat and a yearning she didn't completely understand.

Yet again, she experienced a moment of wishing there could be something more between them, something real, but he was being entirely too heavy-handed. She was a modern woman, not someone who would succumb to a man because she'd been ordered to by another.

At the same time, she reacted to Karim as he bent to kiss her cheek. The corners of her mouth stopped cooperating and went every direction. She thought he drew a deliberate inhale, drinking in the scent of her skin when his face was that close, but he straightened away and she was lost at sea again.

She looked to her hands in her lap, pulse throbbing in her throat and tried to focus on the ring. When she finally saw it clearly, she was utterly taken with it—as she was by all sparkly, pretty things. But it was legitimately loose on her, not even staying on her middle finger without dropping right off.

"I would feel horrible if anything happened to it," she said truthfully to Karim. "Would you please take custody of it until it can be resized?"

"If you prefer."

"Do you mind?" she asked Tahirah before she removed it. "I would be devastated if I lost it. It's so beautiful and means so much to you."

Tahirah looked saddened but nodded. "Of course. It's even loose on me these days. It fit me perfectly through my pregnancy and Karim's childhood, but I haven't had a proper appetite since losing his father. Once I took it off, I couldn't bear to wear it again. It reminded me too starkly of what I'd lost. Everything does."

This was why Karim was marrying Galila, this anguish that his mother still carried three decades after her loss. How could he take the grief she attributed to a tragic accident and reveal that her husband had deliberately left her? That he had thrown himself off a balcony, rather than face life without the *real* object of his love?

Fortunately, Galila asked about the palace and other things, not letting his mother dwell too far in the darkness of the past. Karim had been worried when the topic of her mother had come up as they arrived, but now they were moving on to a recap of her brother's wedding and other harmless gossip.

At a light knock, his mother said, "I've had a luncheon prepared. Shall we go through to my private dining room?"

Galila excused herself to freshen up.

"She seems lovely," his mother said as Galila disappeared.

"She is," Karim said, relieved to discover Galila was so skillful at small talk. Their marriage was expedient, and he had spent a restless night thinking that having her as a wife would be a sexually gratifying, if dangerous, game, but he was seeing potential in her to be the sort of partner who fit into his world as if made for it.

She was royal herself. Of course she understood the niceties and other social finesses that were required, especially with women and the older generation. He wasn't sure he wanted to like her for it, though. He needed his guard up at all times.

A servant started to come in, saw they were still in the parlor and quickly made apologies for interrupting them, turning to exit just as quickly.

He noticed what the girl held and waved her to come in and attend to her task.

"Haboob?" he asked his mother as the maid crouched to set the seals in place around the door

onto the balcony. He'd been too distracted this morning to check the weather, but the dust storms came up very suddenly, which was probably why his pilot hadn't said anything.

"I'll have rooms prepared for you," his mother said, taking his arm as he led her into her private dining room. It overlooked the oasis next to which the palace was built. The wind was already tugging at the fronds of the palms and whirling sand into small devils.

"I need to return to Nabata this afternoon. Perhaps we'll skip the meal—" He glanced up as a different servant appeared, wide-eyed and anxiously wringing her hands. Thankfully, she stood behind his mother so his mother didn't see her.

Karim knew instantly what the trouble was. Galila should have rejoined them by now. He scratched his cheek, not revealing his instantaneous fury.

"You'll have to excuse us, Mother. We'll stay ahead of the storm. I hope you'll join us in Nabata very soon and have a proper chance to get to know Galila before the wedding."

"Of course," she said with disappointment. "Be careful. I should say goodbye."

"No need." He kissed her cheek and strode from the room, taking the maid into the hall with him. He asked which car Galila had taken, then hurried outside the palace to snap his fingers at his pilot.

They had to catch his runaway princess before she was caught in the coming storm.

CHAPTER THREE

GALILA'S GETAWAY WAS an exhilarating race down a straight stretch of paved road through the desert. If the sun seemed to dim, she blamed the tinted windows, not her mood. She didn't have any gloomy feelings about leaving Karim. Zero. She couldn't do it fast enough.

Then the light pouring through the sunroof really did change. It became a strobing flash as a helicopter hovered over the car, casting its shadow on the hood. The *rat-a-tat* chop of the blades cut into the otherwise luxuriously silent interior.

"So what?" she shouted. "I have a full tank and an open road."

She would get herself to the border into Khalia and once there, she would be her own person again. She would fly to Europe and stay there.

Pull a Malak and quit the family. Do whatever the hell she wanted.

She jammed her foot even harder onto the accelerator. The road was straight and clear, not another car in sight.

He raced ahead, staying low, then stopped and landed in the middle of the road.

"Bastard!"

She had half a mind to ram the car straight into him. With a muted scream of frustration through gritted teeth, she lifted her foot from the accelerator.

As her speed dropped off, she searched for a way around the helicopter, but it blocked both lanes. This car wouldn't get very far off-road, unfortunately. The soil might look hard-packed, but pockets of loose sand could swallow a tire in a heartbeat. This was the sort of sedan built for a paved highway, not scrubby desert. It would spin in the dirt until it ran out of fuel.

Turn around? The only place to go was back to his mother's palace.

Oh, she was frustrated as she braked! She came

to a reluctant stop as she reached the helicopter while its blades were still rotating.

She flung herself from the car. The wash off the rotors caught at her hair. She used a finger to drag it out of her eyes.

"I *will not* marry you," she shouted in single-syllable blurts when Karim came out of the helicopter, expression thunderous.

"Look," he said with a stabbing point to her left.

That was when she realized why the sky had been growing darker. A red-brown cloud rose like a tsunami against the sky. *Haboob.*

She didn't normally swear out loud, so she swallowed the words threatening to fall from her lips.

"We'll outrun it. I want to be in Nabata when it hits." Karim threw his arm around her, using his body to shield her as best he could while he more or less dragged her toward the helicopter.

Much as she wanted to fight him, windstorms could be deadly.

"What about the car?" she shouted.

His pilot was already leaping out of his seat. Galila presumed he would take the vehicle back to the palace and allowed Karim to push her into the copilot's seat.

"This isn't an agreement to marry you," she told him as she buckled in and accepted the headphones he handed her.

He ignored her statement as he quickly buckled in himself and put on his own headset. Maybe he didn't hear her. He lifted off in seconds, perfectly adept as a pilot, which was kind of sexy, not that she wanted to notice.

Within moments, they were racing toward the rocky hills in the distance.

She eyed him, trying to gauge how angry he was. It was difficult to tell when his body seemed to move with natural precision and that stern mouth of his had probably never smiled. She hadn't expected to get caught so she hadn't worried too much about his reaction to her escape, but he wasn't her father and her brothers.

Until this morning, she had been confident she could cajole nearly anything out of anyone—

schooling in Europe, Thoroughbred horses, designer clothing. When it came to her charity work, she was a money-raising machine, squeezing record donations out of men and women alike. With very few exceptions, she always got what she wanted.

Things had changed, however. Her stupid brother had put her at the mercy of this wretched man and Karim didn't strike her as the indulgent sort, his mother's remarks notwithstanding. In fact, the longer she watched him, the more her uneasiness grew.

He swore, sudden and sharp as a gunshot, loud enough to make her jump because it came into her head through the earmuffs, crystal clear. For one second, she thought the curse had been aimed at her, then he made a sudden veering motion that tilted them as he avoided something.

She looked forward where visibility had become severely reduced. Despite his efforts, the storm was wrapping around them, buffeting the helicopter. They were running out of time. And options.

He went lower, searching for a safe place to land, but the rotor wash kicked up more dust, making it nearly impossible to see what was on the ground.

"There!" she said as she saw a flash of blue and green, black and yellow—colors and symmetries that didn't belong in the rust-red of the desert. It was a Bedouin camp, men running around securing tents and corralling the camels.

Karim set down on the nearest flat piece of land and turned off the engine, but the rotors continued to turn and whine.

"I have to tie down. Wait here." He leaped from the helicopter.

One of the Bedouins clutched his head-covering and ran to greet him. She saw the shock and flash of a wide smile of recognition before the man hurried to help, shouting at one of his fellow tribesmen that their sheikh was among them.

"Tell the women," she heard him shout. To prepare food and suitable lodging, Galila surmised.

She pulled off her headphones and drew the scarf from around her neck to drape it over her head and prepare to wrap it across her face. Zyria wasn't a country where face covering was demanded, but she would have to protect herself from the blast of dust.

That was when she realized her purse was in the car and she didn't have her sunglasses. Her toothbrush was with her luggage, though.

She went through to the passenger cabin, having to catch her balance twice because the wind was trying so hard to knock the helicopter off its footings. The luggage compartment was easily accessed and she quickly retrieved her necessities along with stealing the shaving kit out of Karim's case. Such things were always the last into the luggage so it was right on top.

Then she shamelessly dumped his laptop bag onto an empty seat. She began filling it with the contents of the onboard pantry—coffee and tea, fresh oranges and bananas, nuts and dried figs, cheese and crackers, chocolates and Turkish delight. Caviar? Sure. Why not?

"What the hell are you doing?" he bit out as he came through from the cockpit.

"Food." She showed him the bag, swollen with his travel larder. "Our toothbrushes are in here, too. Time to run?" She buttoned her jacket and drew her scarf across her face.

He clearly hadn't expected this. He glanced at her heeled shoes. Yes, well, she hadn't made a priority of digging out her pool sandals. She'd been too busy making herself useful.

The helicopter jerked again. They couldn't stay here. The very thing that kept this bird aloft was liable to topple it in the wind. The Bedouins had spent centuries learning how to wait out these types of storms, however. She and Karim would be safer in one of their tents.

Karim leaped out the side door, not bothering with the steps. He reached back to take her by the hips and lift her to the ground while one of the Bedouins stood by and slammed the door behind her.

She dragged her scarf up to peer through the layer of silk, relying more on Karim's hard arms around her to guide her than the ability to actually see. She had only ever watched a storm through a window. It was terrifying to be in it, making her anxious when Karim pressed her into a tent and left her there.

A handful of women were moving around inside it, efficiently smoothing bright blue sheets and plumping cushions on a low bed, setting out a battery-operated lantern on a small dining rug and urging her to sit at a washing basin.

The walls and roof of the tent fluttered while the wind howled and sand peppered the exterior. She removed her scarf and jacket, grateful to wipe away the worst of the dust with a damp cloth. She wound up changing into the silk nightgown she had thrown into the bag since all of her clothes felt so gritty. It wasn't cold in here, not with the sunbaked earth still radiating heat and so many warm bodies in here, but she accepted the delicate shawl one woman handed her.

The entire camp had been informed that the sheikh's intended bride, the Princess of Khalia, was among them. They were pulling out all the stops, eager to praise her choice of husband.

Choice? Ha!

But they wanted to make her comfortable so Galila bit her tongue. She had done enough work with the underprivileged to understand that her problems were not the sort that most people identified with. These women had chapped hands and tired smiles. Everything they owned, they carried.

She let them fuss over her, rather appreciating the motherly kindness of the old woman who wanted to brush her hair. After she had washed her face and hands, she gave her moisturizer to the old woman. The woman laughed and said nothing could erase her wrinkles, but she was pleased all the same.

The other women were excited by the fresh fruit and other treats, insisting on adding a selection from the bag to Galila's meal of stew and lentils.

That was when Galila realized the dining mat was set for two.

What had Karim told them? They couldn't share this tent! They weren't married.

Karim was their sheikh, however. When he entered the tent, the women scattered with gasps and giggles, not a single protest for Galila's honor.

It was fully dark outside by then, despite the still early hour. The tent was lit only by the small lantern over the meal they would share. The wind howled so loudly, she couldn't hear any voices in the neighboring tents.

Now she realized why the women had been so admiring of this silly nightgown, intent on ensuring her hair was shiny and tangle-free as it flowed around her bare shoulders and fell just so across the lace on her back. That was why they had praised him and called him lucky and said she would make him a good and dutiful wife.

They thought she was consummating her wedding night!

She hugged the delicate shawl more closely around her. Her pulse throbbed in the pit of her belly. She curled her toes into the silk nap of the rug beneath her feet, clammy and hot at the same time. Her mind trailed to the way he'd made her feel last night, kissing her so passionately, while the rest of her fluttered with nerves.

He took a long, leisurely perusal from her loose hair to the hem of her ivory nightgown.

Without a word, he removed his robe and scraped his headwear off, tossing the dust-covered garments aside without regard. He wore a white tunic beneath that he also peeled off, leaving him bare-chested in loose white pants that hung low across his hips. He stepped out of his sandals.

She swallowed.

His mouth might have twitched, but he only turned and knelt with splayed thighs on the bathing mat, using the same cloth she had run down her throat and under her breasts to wash his face and behind his neck.

She shouldn't be watching him. Her pulse raced with a taboo excitement as she gazed on the burnished skin that flexed across his shoulders. Her ears picked up the sound of water being wrung from the cloth, and his quiet sigh of relief. Those sounds did things to her. Her skin tightened and her intimate regions throbbed.

She imagined replacing that cloth with her hands, smoothing soap along the strong arm he raised, running slippery palms up his biceps, over his broad shoulders, down to his chest and rib cage. If she snaked her touch beneath his arm to his navel, would she be able to trace the narrow line of hair she had glimpsed, the one that disappeared into the waistband of his trousers?

What would he look like completely naked? What would he *feel* like?

As wildness threatened to take her over completely, she tried to forestall it by blurting, "You shouldn't be in here."

"Worried about your reputation? We're married." He stayed on the mat with his back to her, continuing to stroke the cloth along his upraised arms and across his chest.

"I don't know how to say this more clearly, but—"

"They have already given up one much-needed tent for me," he interjected, pausing in his bath to speak over her. "I won't ask them to prepare one for you as well. We share this one. Therefore, we must be married. We are."

"Just like that?" she choked. "The sheikh has spoken and thus it is so?"

"Exactly."

She didn't even have words for the weakness that went through her. She told herself it was the deflation of watching her childhood dreams of a royal wedding disappear in a poof, but it was the way her life had changed in the time it took for him to make a declaration.

"You can't." She spoke so faintly she was surprised he heard her.

"It is done, Galila. Accept it." He rinsed the cloth and gave it a hard wring.

"I can't."

She had avoided marriage for many reasons, one of the biggest ones being that she wanted a choice in how she lived her life. At no time had she been satisfied with the idea of putting her fate into the hands of any man—particularly one who didn't love her and didn't seem to even *like* her. She barely knew him!

What she did know was that he was strong and powerful in every way. No one would come to her aid here even if they heard her scream over the wailing wind. In a matter of a few words, he had stripped away all the shields she possessed—her family name, her station as Khalia's only princess, even the composure she had taken years to construct. There was no affection or admiration or infatuation to leverage here. This was all about expediency. About what *he* wanted.

She tightened her fists at her sides, throat aching while the backs of her eyes grew hot, but she refused to let him see she was terrified.

"You are an educated man with intelligence and—I would hope—a shred of honor." Perhaps that wasn't true, considering he'd used her at the wedding and seemed to have no conscience about behaving like a barbarian from centuries ago. Realizing that made her tremble even harder. "You can't just declare us married and force yourself on me."

"I'm not going to attack you," he said sardonically. "Quit sounding like a terrified virgin."

"I *am* a virgin." She spat it out with as much angst as anger.

He froze, then dropped the cloth and rose, pivoting so neatly on the ball of his foot, the rug gathered beneath him into a knot.

"How?" he asked, sounding very casual with his inquiry, but the intensity that seemed to grip him caused the hot coil in her belly to tighten and glow while her heart teetered and shifted. It thumped in wavering beats, unsure whether to feel threatened or excited under his laser-sharp regard.

"What do you mean, 'how'?" She grew prickly with self-consciousness, face scorched even though virginity was nothing to be ashamed of. "The usual way. By not having sex."

"You're twenty-*five*."

"Six."

He gave his head a small shake, as if he didn't understand the words passing between them.

"How have you not been with a man?"

"I've dated. Had boyfriends. I'm not...completely inexperienced." None of her relationships had lasted, though, because she didn't put out. Not much, anyway. She confined things to kissing and a bit of petting. She knew what happened between the sheets. Girlfriends had described the process in profound detail over the years, which truth be told, hadn't always been a selling feature. The process sounded both incredibly intimate and kind of ridiculous.

"Weren't you curious?"

"Sure." She shrugged, trying to appear offhand when this conversation was equally intimate and awkward. "But not enough to sleep with a man just to know what happens. It's not a book where you can skip to the end and make sure it will satisfy before you wade through all the exposition."

He made a noise that might have been a choke of amusement, but his face remained a mask of astonishment.

"What?" she demanded. She had wanted more. So much more than the tepid feelings that most men inspired in her. Even when her suitors had been adoring and dazzled by her, it hadn't been enough. She hadn't trusted their infatuation to last. She needed *more*.

Karim hung his hands off his hips. "You were

going to take me to your room last night," he reminded.

"I was drunk," she claimed, even though with him, it had been different. She had felt the "more" that she'd been craving. At least, she'd thought she had. Now she was so confused, she didn't know what she felt.

He barked out a single harsh, "Ha!" and came toward her.

She stumbled backward in alarm only to have him catch at her arms and steady her.

"You're about to step into our dinner."

She shrugged off his touch, disturbed by the way her whole body was now tingling, and lowered to the rug with him, the food between them.

He stretched out on his side, propped on an elbow. His stern face relaxed a smidge. Maybe. She watched him closely, but wasn't sure.

"Are you laughing at me?"

"No." He reached for an olive in a dish. "Us, maybe. I don't care for lies," he stated. "Tell me now if it's not true. You're really a virgin?"

In the low light, his eyes were more black pupil

than brown iris as his gaze came up to take hold of her own, refusing to let it go.

"I am," she said, wondering why her voice had retreated behind a veil and came out shy and wispy. She cleared her throat, searching for the confident woman who usually occupied her skin. "Are you?"

"No." Flat and unapologetic.

She managed to break their stare by rolling her eyes. She had fully expected that answer, but a pang struck in her chest all the same. Jealous? That would be a ridiculous response when she kind of hated him.

Didn't she?

He ate another olive, still watching her. "Be thankful I'm familiar with writing compelling exposition."

"Don't be smug." The pang went through her again. She wanted to splay her hand over his face and give him a firm shove.

His mouth twitched. "You've been living in Europe for years. I would have thought you would have been drunk before last night."

She had, but she ignored the dig inside his comment and asked, "How do you know where I've been living?"

He shrugged. His gaze lowered to scan the food, but it seemed like a subterfuge.

"Big fan of gossip sites, are you?" she prompted.

"My advisors have kept you on my list of prospects for years. Ours has always been seen as an advantageous match. I would have thought it had been viewed that way in Khalia as well. Your father never suggested me when discussing your own marriage plans? Frankly, I'm surprised you're still single, never mind a virgin."

"Names came up, yours among them," she admitted. "I wasn't interested in marrying so I never bothered to look at photos or read any of the advisements I was sent. Being in Europe, I didn't attend many events to meet any bachelors, either. My mother always sided with me that I didn't have to hurry into marriage."

"That seems odd. Why not?"

Galila shrugged, curling her knees under her, trying to get comfortable but feeling as though she sat on sharp stones. It wasn't the ground beneath the floor of the tent, however. It was the rocky relationship with her mother that was poking at her.

Karim reached a long arm to the bed and handed her a cushion.

"Thank you," she murmured and shoved it under her hip.

"Your mother didn't encourage any match? Or just not ours?" He seemed to watch her with hawk-like attention.

"It wasn't personal." She told herself she was reading more intense interest from him than the topic warranted because she was feeling so sensitive. She took her time arranging her nightgown so it covered her feet, not wanting him to read the layers of mixed feelings she carried when it came to her mother. They were far too close to the bone to share with a stranger. She wasn't drunk tonight, and she had learned the hard way that he used every weakness for his own gain. "She was sensitive to the signs of age. Preferred to put off being called Grandmother as long as possible."

It hadn't been about her daughter's well-being, but it had suited Galila to avoid the shackles so she had been grateful.

He made a noncommittal noise and accepted the bowl of stew she served him.

"Karim," she said, boldly using his name and finding it a caress in her throat. "I am a modern woman with a liberal education. You cannot expect me to give you my virginity simply because you declare us married."

"Galila." Somehow, he sounded as if he mocked her solemnity, yet turned her own name into an endearment. "You caught fire in my arms when your senses were dulled by alcohol. Your sober brain is now regretting your impulsiveness, but I expect we'll be even more combustible when we lie together. You will give me your virginity because you want to."

She couldn't move, felt caught in amber, her whole being suffused with thick honey that suffocated with the aim of creating something eternal.

"I had hoped that would be tonight," he added in a voice that seemed to roll into her ears from far away, barely discernible over the noise outside the swaying walls of this tent. "But your inexperience changes things. We'll wait for your trust in me to grow. I've given my staff two weeks to arrange a wedding ceremony and reception at the palace. We can wait until then."

She choked. A whole two weeks? Wow.

"How am I *ever* supposed to trust you when you tricked me into this?" she asked, voice cracking with emotion. "How am I supposed to feel confident—proud—to be your queen when I'm only a strategic political move?"

That was his cue to profess a deeper interest in her as a woman. It wouldn't be a lie to say he was intrigued by the facets she kept revealing. He had thought her impulsive and spoiled, not given to thinking of others. That was certainly the impression she had left last night. Her brother's disparagement of her actions this morning had more or less confirmed it.

But she had put his mother at ease and it didn't escape him that she had ensured the family ring stayed in his possession while she plotted her foiled escape.

He had been prepared to let loose with his riled temper when he confronted her on the highway, but she hadn't kicked up a fuss at their emergency takeoff. She had evacuated with as much awareness of their danger as required. She wasn't balking at camping with the Bedouins, either. Instead of acting like she was above these rough conditions, she had ensured they contributed to the community food supply, guaranteeing she reflected well on him and the union he had made and knowing full well it would affect his country in subtle, unalterable ways.

The worst complaint he had so far was that she had cost him a favored laptop bag, since he wouldn't dream of asking for its return. Even her escape had worked to his advantage, providing him a reason to shift their marriage from intended to a *fait accompli*. He had been on fire since he had spoken the words.

Now he had discovered she was a virgin? He had neither expected nor particularly wanted an untouched bride, but having one was an inordinate thrill. A primal possessiveness gripped him, chest and belly and groin. He would be the only man to stroke and taste and mate with her. She was *his*.

His inner barbarian howled with triumph, recalling the way she had ignited in his arms, demanding to stoke that blaze into an all-consuming inferno *now*.

The very fact he hovered so close to losing his rational brain to the primal one, however, told him he had to slow things down. For her sake and his own.

So he was careful to keep his tone even, not betraying how craven desire licked like flames inside him. "You're very beautiful, Galila. Of course I desire you."

Every man she had ever come into contact with must have desired her. It defied comprehension that she had never physically shared herself with one of them. He wasn't in the habit of disbelieving people, but he genuinely couldn't understand how a woman of her naturally sensual nature hadn't indulged her passion to its fullest extent. *He* had.

Or rather, he had always believed he had. She might have already reset the bar—which was yet another disturbing layer to this thing between them.

All of these thoughts he held to himself behind an impervious mask.

She studied him, picking apart his words and seeming to grow more and more skeptical of them as the seconds passed.

"My beauty has nothing to do with this. You don't care if I'm beautiful. You're beautiful. Do you want me to believe you chose me so we can make beautiful babies?"

He felt his eyebrows jump. The topic of an heir hadn't entered his mind beyond the abstract, but now she had brought it up...

"We should talk about that."

"How beautiful you are?"

"Children."

She scowled and shifted to hug her knees. "Politically expedient broodmare. Is that what I am? How romantic. A thousand times yes, I wish to be your wife, Karim."

He ought to curtail that sarcasm. No one else in their right mind would speak with such casual disrespect toward him, but he found her temper revealing. She probably didn't realize how much of her genuine thoughts and emotions she betrayed with that barbed tongue of hers.

"You had other plans for your life? Tell me how I've derailed them. Perhaps there's a compromise."

"Yes, you strike me as a man who compromises all the time."

Ah. That was what she was afraid of.

"I rarely have to," he admitted. "From the time I was old enough to grasp an adult conversation, I sat with my father in his meetings. He died when I was six and my uncle continued to include me in every decision he made on my behalf, explaining his reasoning. By the time I was fourteen, I was effectively running the country with his guidance and support. *He* carried out *my* wishes until I was officially crowned."

She blinked wide eyes at him. "Zufar is barely ready for that level of responsibility at thirty-three."

"He has the luxury of a father who still lives."

She cocked her head with curiosity. "What happened to your father? It was an accident, wasn't it? I don't recall exactly."

"He fell from a balcony at the palace." He repeated the lie by rote, even though it grated on him to this day that he was forced to carry such a dark secret. He hated lies, probably because his father had burdened him with such earth-shattering ones. "He'd been drinking."

"Ah," she said with soft compassion. "That's why you were so disparaging. I see now why you resent anyone who fails to appreciate the destructive power of alcohol."

He resented a lot of things—his father's affair with her mother, her mother for leaving his father and causing his father to pursue a desperate act. Now Karim learned there had been a child?

It wasn't as though he hadn't considered that possibility over the years—and again in the last twenty-four hours specifically where Galila was concerned. She had been born long after his father had died, however. There was no chance they were related, which was quite possibly the only bright spot in this otherwise three-act tragedy.

"Do you want to tell me about him?" she invited gently.

"No." He didn't regret his abrupt response. He rarely spoke about his father, but the way she closed up like a flower, showing him her stony profile, caused him to sigh internally.

Women. They were as delicate as thin-skinned fruit, bruising at the least thing.

"Your father left you without a choice," she summed up, still not looking at him. "So you're comfortable imposing a lack of choice on others."

He wasn't so soft he felt stung by that remark, but he did feel it, maybe because the fact she was striking out that hard told him how deeply her own resentment ran at what he was demanding of her.

"You weren't planning to avoid marriage forever, were you?" People in their position couldn't.

"I was waiting to fall in love."

Ah. Something like regret moved in him, but he wanted there to be no false hopes between them.

"It's true that I will never expect or offer you love," he agreed. "That particular emotion is as treacherous and devastating as alcohol."

"You've been in love?" Her pupils exploded as though she'd taken a punch.

"No. Like alcohol, I don't need to imbibe to see the inherent risks and have the sense to avoid it."

A small flinch and her lashes swept down, mouth pouted.

"It doesn't mean we can't have a successful marriage. In fact, going into this union with realistic expectations ensures we won't be disappointed in the long run."

"Is that what you think?" She took a cube of cheese. "Because the problem isn't whether you can grow to love me. It's that I expected to choose my own husband, not have one forced upon me. I *expected* to make a family when it felt right, because I wanted to see something of my husband in the children I made. If you give me sons and daughters, I'm sure I'll love them, but I don't desire your children."

That one did land in a previously unknown vulnerability. Why?

"Meanwhile, you expect me to give up my freedom so you won't have to go through the inconvenience of renegotiating a few trade agreements with the new Sheikh of Khalia. The two most important decisions any woman will make are whom she will marry and whether she will have children. You expect to make both of those decisions for me. That's not fair."

"As I said, we can talk about children." He wasn't a monster. He had already said they could curtail the sex, hadn't he?

"You still expect me to breed with you eventually," she said with a sharp angst. "You gain on every level with this marriage and I gain nothing. In fact, I lose everything. And I'm not even allowed to feel disappointed? *Your* expectations are the ones that are too high, Karim."

CHAPTER FOUR

"I CAN GIVE you pleasure."

The wind had died down, the light was off, and the sound of a gently plucked string on a *rababeh* carried from one of the other tents. They weren't expected to appear before morning so they had turned in early. Galila had formed a dam down the center of the mattress with a rolled mat and a few cushions before asking Karim which side he wanted.

"Everything that happens in bed between us will be your choice," was his response.

She had sat there stunned by what sounded like a vow, trying to understand why she felt both moved and overwhelmed. It felt like too much responsibility for a woman who knew so little about the things she might want from her marriage bed.

And now, in the darkest dark, he was telling her he could teach her.

She wanted to say something cynical but couldn't find any words, let alone form them with her dry mouth and even drier throat.

"Are you awake?" he asked in a quieter voice.

"Yes." She probably should have stayed silent and let him think she had missed hearing what he said, but she revealed her wakefulness and died a little inside. She threw her wrist across her eyes, wanting to go back thirty hours or so and never take a single sip of brandy at her brother's wedding.

The silence between them grew with expectation.

"I can give myself pleasure," she pointed out, glad for the dark so he wouldn't see her blush at the admission she was making.

Silence was his answer, but she swore she could hear him smiling.

"Don't even pretend you don't…" She couldn't finish the sentence.

"Read the footnotes?" he suggested.

"Oh, yes, you're a delight in bed. So glad I can share this one with you." She turned her back on him and clenched her eyes shut. Her fist knotted in the edge of the blanket and nestled it tight under her chin.

After a pensive few minutes, he said, "I had to take advantage of the opportunity you presented me, Galila."

"Yes, well, I'm not presenting one now. Perhaps give me some quiet so I can get my beauty sleep."

"For various reasons, I never thought you and I would be a good fit, despite the fact my advisors consistently brought you to my attention. You seemed young, wayward and superficial."

"Are you sure you're not a virgin? Because you're offering very little pleasure with remarks like that."

"No one else appealed to me, though." He sounded almost as if this was a surprise revelation only occurring to him now, one that dismayed him. He sounded disturbed, even.

She sighed. "Please don't make this about my

looks, Karim. That's no better than using me for political gain."

"I didn't come to the wedding intending to make an offer for you. I wouldn't have kissed you if you hadn't kissed me first. But when we did…"

"Karim." She was glad for the dark because she was wincing with mortified agony. "I know you weren't as involved as I was. I felt your…" She swallowed. "Distance. Before we were seen."

"That only proves how attuned we are to one another. Physically."

"No! It proves you can manipulate me with my body while I have no such power over you."

He shifted abruptly, voice now coming from the space above and behind her shoulder, telling her he was propped on an elbow. "Did you want me to lose myself and make love to you against the wall where everyone could see us?"

"I wanted you not to use me!"

"I'm offering you a chance to use me."

"You're not that simplistic. Or generous. You're going to get me all worked up, then say, 'Why don't we go all the way?' Not my first rodeo, cowboy."

"Am I?"

"What?"

"Going to get you all worked up? Because I know how to settle myself down. You have no fear I'll prevail on you to provide *my* happy ending."

"Oh!" She buried her cry of frustration into her pillow. "Fine," she declared with the impulsiveness that had earned her a reputation for being exactly as spoiled and wayward as everyone thought her. "Go ahead and prove there's something in this marriage for me. Give me all this pleasure you're so convinced you can provide."

Nothing. No compliments or commands. He didn't move.

She suspected he still hovered over her, but it was too dark to tell. She turned to face him, one hand inching just enough to feel the silk tassel on the cushion still between them.

He drew the rolled mat out of the way and his

hand bumped hers when he sought the cushion. He kept hold of her hand.

She didn't know what to do. Pull away? Let her hand rest in his? She was nervous. Curious. Furious. Frustrated in more ways than one.

He lifted her hand and rubbed his lips against her knuckle. The short whiskers of his closely trimmed beard were silky soft where the backs of her fingers brushed against them.

"This isn't about how you look, Galila," he breathed across her skin. "I can't see you. It's about how we make each other feel."

"How do you feel?"

His humid breath bathed her palm before he spoke into it. "I'll let you know when you get there."

The light play of his mouth exploring her skin, the dampness when he opened his lips, sent heady tingles through her entire body. When he pressed a kiss into her palm and set his blazingly hot mouth against the inside of her wrist, tongue swirling against her pulse, she gasped at the wave of arousal that throbbed through her. It sent heaviness into her loins, stinging tightness to the tips of her breasts, and a helpless sob to catch in her throat.

"How are you doing this to me?" He was touching her *hand*.

"What am I doing? Tell me. I can't see you."

"You're—" She didn't want to admit he was seducing her. "I can't breathe. My heart feels like I've run miles."

He moved her hand to his neck, setting the heel of her palm against his smooth throat, next to where his Adam's apple moved as he swallowed. The artery there held a powerful pulse, one that was quick and hard.

"You're excited?" she asked.

"Of course."

No. He was tricking her again. But she found herself doing what she had last night, acting out of instinct, but this time her fingers were in his thick, silky hair. She urged him down and somehow their mouths found each other despite the blinding darkness.

The lack of light amplified the acuteness of her

senses. Such a rush of heat went into her lips, her mouth stung under his, assuaged by the lazy way he settled into the kiss, easing her lips to part. She was the one to seek a deeper kiss by searching for his tongue with her own and moaned as their kiss grew fully involved.

His arm snaked around her and he tucked her half beneath him, weight settling more heavily on her. Then he lifted his head just enough to say, "Say yes," against her lips.

He wanted this to be her choice and it was. His bare chest pressed where the straps of her nightgown left her upper chest bare and she had never felt anything like that specific heat and texture. It was intoxicating.

"Yes," she whispered, arching to pull her hair out from beneath her.

It brushed against his skin, and he made a noise that suggested he had to reach for restraint.

"This might become my obsession," he said, gathering the long waves and burying his face in it. When he turned his head, his mouth was against her nape. He licked into the hollow beneath her ear and sucked on her earlobe, making her whimper in delight.

His touch moved to play his barely there fingertips against the silk of her nightgown, following the band of lace beneath her breasts where it hid her navel, coming back to climb the slippery silk alongside the swell of her breast. By the time his touch met where his lips had strayed, and he began to ease the narrow strap down her shoulder, her breasts were swollen and aching. She was so needy, she was feeling wild. Her own hands were moving restlessly across his shoulders, excited but apprehensive.

"I'm going to make love to you with my mouth," he said in a voice that barely penetrated the rush of blood in her ears. "That's not a pleasure you can give yourself."

Was that what she wanted? She didn't know, but she was too caught up in the sensation of his beard across the top of her breast. He bared it and she stopped being able to think straight. The heat of his breath warned her just before his mouth engulfed her nipple, but nothing could have prepared her for the way electricity seemed to shoot through her, stabbing into her heart so she thought it would burst. Sexual need raced in sharp lines to her loins, making her tingle and tremble as he pulled and laved and cupped the swell in his big hand and flicked his tongue against the turgid tip.

She could feel herself growing damp and slick. Heard wanton noises escaping her throat. She wanted him to keep sucking her nipples, but wanted to kiss him, too. It was the sweetest torture and she actually lifted and offered herself when he eased the other strap down, desperate for the delicious torture on her other breast.

Oh, he was making her crazy. She swirled her hands through his hair, over his damp neck, across his shoulders. The dip of his spine was an intriguing place and she even wickedly slipped her hand down to touch his chest, finding his own nipples sharp as shards of glass.

He rose to kiss her mouth again, hard and thorough. She moaned her approval, body rolling into his of its own volition, knee crooking.

When he ran his hand down her hip, he pushed the blankets away at the same time. Then he gathered the skirt of her nightgown, drawing it up so her legs felt the cool night air. It was erotic and almost a relief, she was so hot, but it was a moment of truth. Was this really what she wanted?

The darkness was a wonderful place, allowing her to hide and somehow protect her modesty as his touch strayed inward and brushed the damp hair between her thighs. He caressed her swollen lips, more of tease, so entrancing she allowed her thighs to relax open.

He didn't get the message and continued being so gentle, she wanted to sob with frustration. She was nothing but an agony of anticipation, waiting, longing, yearning for a firmer touch.

He shifted and slid down, pressed her legs wider, beard brushing the sensitive skin of her inner thigh, sweeping in brush strokes that made her gasp and quiver with need. When he turned his face against one thigh and the other, refusing to make contact where she pulsed with molten heat, she sobbed, "Karim."

"You want my mouth here?" His wide palm settled on her mound, the pressure not nearly firm enough.

He wanted her full surrender. She instinctively knew this wasn't compromise. It was his way of forcing her to accept his will, but it was such a wickedly delicious way. Seductive. Impossible to resist.

"I do," she admitted, feeling as though she gave herself up to him with the words, binding herself irrevocably to him. "I do, I do."

Openmouthed kisses edged closer. He parted her with delicate care, then wet heat slid along her most intimate flesh. Glittering pleasure suffused her, waves of growing arousal that rose as his attentions deepened. In fact, her level of involvement skyrocketed so fast and high, she didn't know how to handle it.

He paused, causing her to open her mouth in a silent scream of agony. Only his hot breath caressed her as he spoke in a graveled tone.

"Use your words, my pretty bird. I can't tell if

you're struggling because you don't like it or you like it too much."

"Too much," she gasped. "So much. Please. Keep going."

He held her thighs open with firm hands, muting the buck of her hips as he took his time, seeming to recognize when she was on the brink of climax, then slowing to hold her on that plateau, forcing her to languish in that place of mindlessly unbearable perfection.

She stroked her fingers into his hair again, thinking this was ridiculous and far too personal, but she didn't care. She only wanted him to keep doing this forever, yet she could barely withstand the intensity of this pleasure. Not much longer. Couldn't. Absolutely couldn't bear it.

He pressed his mouth over her with firm possession, causing her to hit the crest of her wave with a cry of loss and triumph. Her entire body shuddered as the climax rolled through her in powerful waves.

He remained attentive, ensuring every last pulse was teased to its fullest degree, until she was spent and splayed, panting in the dark. She felt the dampness on her lashes against the arm she threw over her eyes. Yes, that had been so good, she had wept from the power of it.

He lifted away from her but remained between her legs so she couldn't close them. She was aware of his rapid movements, heard his shaken breath, then his long, jagged, relieved sigh.

She dropped her arm and blinked, trying to see him in the absolute dark.

"Did you—?"

"Yes." He stretched out beside her.

She felt a little cheated. Her hands itched to explore him.

He only turned her so she was spooned into his front. Her nightgown was still up around her hips, but he stopped her from trying to pull it down between them.

"Let me feel you against me." His hand smoothed up her hip, then down to settle on her abdomen. His lips touched her shoulder. "Think about how good it will be when I'm inside you and we come together."

When? Did he really want to wait until after their formal ceremony?

The naked contact with him was delicious. In fact, latent desire made the flesh of her mound tingle at the proximity of his hand. He might have given himself release, but he was still firm against her bare buttocks and she was already wondering how it would feel to have him moving inside her while she shattered. She didn't know if she wanted to wait until tomorrow morning, let alone two weeks from now.

Which had no doubt been his plan all along. Ruthless, vexing man.

His arm around her grew heavy as he relaxed into sleep, but she continued to blink into the darkness. She was starting to realize the power she had handed him by letting him take her to such heights. He was in her head now, making her eager to feel exactly what he had suggested. Him, moving inside her while they shattered in unison. He was making her want what he willed.

How would she take herself back from that?

* * *

Karim left his wife sleeping soundly beneath the light blanket. He was hard as titanium, more than primed to fully consummate his marriage, but *he* was master of himself. Not her. Not this need he had stoked by pleasuring her last night.

It was a toss-up as to which of them had enjoyed that more, much to his consternation. Had it been self-indulgent to offer himself like that? Absolutely. When he had settled beside her, he had had no intention of touching her.

But he did want this marriage to work. He did expect progeny from her. And yes, maybe his ego had been stinging from that remark she'd made about not desiring his children. He had definitely wanted to remind her that she desired *him*. That there was something he offered her that no one else could.

Maybe he had needed to prove it to himself, a dark voice whispered. Maybe he had wanted to prove he could pleasure her without losing command of himself—which he very nearly had. If she had invited him to deflower her, he would have been lost completely.

No, all he had proved last night was that the sexual connection between them was so potent, he couldn't entirely trust himself to be alone with her. It was exactly the depth of irrational passion he refused to succumb to the way his father had.

He *would* wait until they were formally married, if only to prove he could.

To that end, he steeled himself and stepped out to the cool morning air, found clean clothes for both of them in the helicopter, then did his pre-flight check while tribesmen brushed the sand off the blades and footings. He was drinking coffee with the men on the far side of the camp when Galila emerged from their tent in the linen pants and T-shirt the women had taken in to her.

Her gaze scanned the encampment until she found him. Pink stained her cheeks and sensual memory softened her expression. Her tentative smile invited him to smile back.

It took everything in him to stay rooted where he was and not cross to touch her. A nearly overwhelming pull urged him to move forward and press her back into their tent for the kind of love-making that drummed like a beat in his groin. A kiss, at least.

He confined himself to a cool nod of acknowledgment.

He was already glancing away when he saw her expression stiffen. He glanced back and her lashes had swept down. She quickly gave her attention to some children who approached, but her cheer seemed forced. She didn't look his way again as she was drawn into the circle of women and children.

His blood stayed hot with memory as he watched her. Her response to him had been exquisite. Explosive. Everything he could want in a wife—if he wasn't a man who knew there was a high cost to high passion. Seducing her had been a pleasure and a strategic move, but it had also been something that could all too easily take him over if he wasn't careful.

He watched her charm that side of the encampment as he continued his discussion with the elders in this tribe.

Karim might not have known Adir al-Zabah was his half brother, but he had heard the name through the years. Adir was renowned in the desert for his toughness and strong leadership, very much revered among the nomads. They couldn't tell Karim what family Adir had come from, however. His parents were unknown.

They asked why he was inquiring, but he brushed aside his questions as idle curiosity. The burden of secrets was his alone to carry.

The way the women and children adulated her was a much-needed balm to Galila's ego after Karim had barely acknowledged her this morning. She knew it was pathetic that she drank up this sort of starstruck wonder like water, but it filled a hollow spot her mother had carved with the hot-cold sway of her affections.

Sometimes Galila wondered if her desire for validation and appreciation ran deeper than that, and was a shared character flaw she had inherited from her mother. Perhaps it wasn't just an enjoyment of being recognized, but an expectation of glorification. Her mother had always acted as if the way her husband doted on her was natural and something to which she was entitled.

That certainly wasn't something Galila could anticipate from *her* husband, she acknowledged with a clench of hurt when he sent a young boy over to relay the message that it was time to leave.

She made promises to the women of supplies and aid as she said goodbye, enjoying the way they blessed her and touched her arms, asked her to kiss a baby and pray for a good marriage for the unmarried girls among them.

Karim waited until they were airborne and waving down at the Bedouins before speaking to her. They were connected via the microphone on the headsets again, making the communication feel almost more like a phone call. "You don't have to send anything. I asked the men. They don't need anything."

She heard something like her brothers' disparaging cynicism in his tone. *They* didn't buy regard with magnanimous acts the way she seemed to try to.

"It is a mark of pride among them, I'm sure, to insist that they meet the needs of their women without help," she responded. "It's little things. Teething gel for the boy who was crying. Feminine supplies for the young girl who is too embarrassed to ask for it. Things that aren't easy to come by out here. If you don't want to pay for it, I will." She had ample funds that had been set aside for her as part of her marriage contract.

"Of course, I'll pay for it," Karim said impatiently.

She curled the corner of her mouth. All men were created equal when it came to impugning their pride, apparently.

He didn't realize how happy she was to spend other people's money on the needs of the less fortunate, however.

She quickly accepted his offer, adding, "I would appreciate very much if I could say you underwrote the things I send, since I also want to include some books for the girls. There seems to be controversy as to whether education is for all the children. It would go a long way if you made it clear you expect everyone to learn to read, not just the boys."

"I do." He wore a scowl as they approached the outskirts of Nabata, as if the remark struck a nerve.

Someone hailed him and he relayed an expected time of arrival, then returned to speaking to her.

"I realize we've fallen behind our neighbors in some ways. When my father was alive, my mother spearheaded women and children initiatives, but she has largely been not much more than a figurehead since his death. Without strong leadership, things have stagnated, rather than continuing to progress. Would you take up that mantle?"

Her first instinct was to leap on the opportunity. In Khalia, she had been her mother's envoy, often earning the credit but not receiving it. There were many times when she hadn't agreed with her mother's decisions, but had had to go along with her because she was a loyal subject of the queen and a dutiful daughter.

"Would I have to run everything by you?" she asked.

"Is that so unreasonable? I'm all for advancements, Galila, but at a pace people can adapt to."

She supposed that was fair, but: "Are you just offering me this role because you know I like it? As a way to persuade me into accepting our marriage?"

"What I offered last night wasn't enough?" he asked in a silky tone that caused a shiver to trickle down her spine.

She refused to look at him.

A moment later, he clicked a button and spoke again to the voice she presumed was at the landing pad. The palace appeared and captured all her attention.

It was clearly the product of centuries of additions. The highest dome dominated the center structure while annexes stretched in four directions, each with a variety of smaller domes, flat roofs, solar panels and even an arch of solarium windows over a great hall of some kind. From each of these four legs grew smaller additions, apartments perhaps—there were a number of small pools and courtyards with palms and fountains.

He landed in a circle on one of the highest rooftops where three other helicopters of various sizes were already tethered. They were hanging their headphones on the hooks above the windscreen when he spoke again.

"How you come to terms with our marriage is up to you, but it is a fact. You may weigh in on the details of our celebration as you see fit, but my staff is perfectly capable of making it happen without your input. As for representing the women of my country—*our* country—I would like you to be their voice, if you're willing. Is that something you would enjoy or not?"

She hesitated, drew a breath and admitted, "Each time I say yes to you, I feel a piece of me fall away. It's not the same for you, though, is it?"

People were approaching to tether the helicopter, but he didn't look away from her, only said a quiet, "No."

It hurt a lot more than she had braced herself for, pushing a thickness into her throat and a pressure behind her eyes.

"Is this still about love, Galila? Look at my mother. You don't want that. Be practical and accept this marriage for the beneficial partnership it can be."

To whom? Everyone *but* her.

She was being offered the chance to elevate the living conditions of a country full of women for the low price of her own freedom and the loving marriage she had always promised herself.

"I've never understood how people live without love." Her brothers did, maybe because they hadn't been loved in the first place. She had, though, and maybe that was proof that Karim was right. She had grown addicted to being seen as special and valuable and wanted. Losing her mother's love was still a deep and agonizing wound.

She knew better than to fall into another situation where she was yearning for feelings that weren't there, yet here she was, distantly hoping he would come around and feel something toward her.

"It's not that difficult," Karim replied drily, essentially driving a coffin nail into her heart. "Come. Let me show you our home."

"Well, I guess I don't have a choice, do I? Not unless I want to throw myself off the edge of this roof and end things right now."

"Why would you say that?" His voice lashed at her, quick and snapping sharp as a whip. "Don't ever say anything like that. *Ever.*"

His vehemence had her recoiling in her seat, heart hammering. She recalled with chagrin that his father had fallen from a balcony here. "I didn't mean—"

He cut her off with a chop of his hand through the air between them and disembarked, then impatiently demanded she come out behind him, picking her up and releasing her with abrupt motions.

He exchanged a few words with someone, then

hurried her out of the heat and into the relief of air conditioning where a handful of personnel awaited them, all wearing attentive expressions.

"Cantara." He introduced a middle-aged woman in traditional dress with heavily made-up eyes, a wide smile and a tablet and stylus at the ready. "My mother's assistant, when she's here at the palace. Cantara will show you around and help you hire the staff you need. I'm required elsewhere."

He strode away. The rest of the staff flowed into position behind him like birds in a flock, making him seem to disappear.

She waited, but he didn't look back. Last night's intimacy was forgotten. It certainly hadn't changed anything in *his* agenda.

"I've had tea prepared in your chamber. May I show you there?"

Galila found a polite smile and dutifully followed where she was led.

Karim forced himself not to look back, but he still saw Galila. Heard her.

How did each word she spoke have such power

over him? She loaded a single glance with a thousand emotions, saying, *I've never understood how people live without love*, while a kaleidoscope of despair and confusion, yearning and wistfulness took their turn across her angelic face. Somehow, she caused those feelings to be reflected in him, twisting his conscience at the same time, which was distinctly uncomfortable.

And when he tried to move her past her melancholy, she thrust a knife from a completely unexpected direction, flippantly suggesting she throw herself to her death the way his father had done.

Whatever pangs of guilt had reverberated through him had been slapped out by that statement, sparking his temper with the power of a lightning strike.

That slam of energy had had its roots in a white-hot fear. He would never wish his experience on anyone, certainly could never face witnessing something so traumatic again, but somehow knew it would be especially devastating if she did it.

He'd smacked a hard lid on that sort of talk,

seeing how wary his outburst made her, but he didn't even want her to dare think of doing something so horrific, let alone threaten it.

The entire five-minute conversation had left her limpid eyed and looking abandoned as a child when he left her with an assistant and turned away.

Perhaps she was entitled to some bewilderment. Their lovemaking had been so powerful, he had stooped to reminding her of it himself, unable to dismiss it from his mind. He wanted her to recall every twitch and sigh and caress. It was all he could think about.

But it was completely reckless to let himself be so distracted and preoccupied by carnal desires. He had married her to keep a secret that could rattle swords in both their countries—upend the entire region, even. Not to mention the personal cost to all of them. Her mother's affair was already a sore topic with her and her siblings. He didn't want to force painful discussions on them any more than he wanted them himself.

No. She might open herself to him and offer a

type of pleasure he had never experienced, lure him like a bee to a nectar-laden flower, but he had to remain stoic and indifferent. And after the way she had behaved at the wedding? Getting drunk and spilling what she had to *him*? There was no way he could entrust her with the rest. Too much depended on him keeping their parents' affair a secret.

To do that, he had to keep her contained, yet at a distance. In his palace, in his apartment, but not in his bed. It was best for all their sakes.

CHAPTER FIVE

TEN DAYS LATER, Galila was fed up with being ignored.

Not that she was ever left alone. Rather, maids and clerks and advisors hovered constantly, asking for her preference on *everything*, right down to which side of the gold-plated bathroom tap her cut-crystal toothbrush cup should sit.

She was changed at least four times a day, from silk pajamas to comfortable breakfast wear, then to casually elegant midday wear, then sophisticated evening wear and finally back to pajamas. If she and Karim were entertaining, there might be poolside wraps while amusing the wife of a visiting diplomat, cocktail attire before dressing for dinner or something ceremonial for an official photograph.

They were always entertaining. Or meeting with

some dignitary over a luncheon. Even breakfasts were business meetings, where she and Karim ate across from each other, but staff hovered with tablets and questions, asking for replies on emails and finalizing their schedules for the rest of the day.

The strange part was, she didn't mind the demands. She found it invigorating. There was something both thrilling and satisfying in making seating arrangements or setting a menu or suggesting a blue rug would look better in this room, and seeing her wishes carried out promptly and without question.

As a princess in Khalia, she had had influence, but even Malak's disinterested male opinions had held more sway than her own. She had nearly always been contradicted by her mother, which Galila had sometimes thought was purely a desire on her mother's part to reinforce her own position, not a genuine partiality to whatever suggestion of Galila's she had decided to overrule.

Now, as Queen of Zyria—and that title made her choke on hysterical laughter because she had yet to properly sleep with her husband, the king—Galila discovered the power of her position. At first, she'd been tentative, expecting to hear that the Queen Mother Tahirah ought to be consulted or had always preferred this or that.

To her amazement, Galila was assured that such courtesies as consulting the Queen Mother were at her discretion. The only voice that might veto her own was her husband's. What a heady thought!

So she tested the extent of her privilege. She sought out her husband unannounced and said she would wait for the king in his anteroom.

She was not turned away. She was offered refreshments. His highest-ranking assistant offered to interrupt the king's conference call if it was an urgent matter.

"It's not. Merely a private discussion I'd like to have before our guests arrive. I'll ring if I require anything."

She was left alone to explore the private library. It was a retreat, a place for Zyria's ruler to freshen up between meetings, since there was a very luxurious bathroom and a small walk-in closet with a spare of everything.

It ought to smell like Karim in here, she thought, as she lifted the sleeve of a robe to her nose.

She was actually craving the scent of him, some lingering evidence of their intimacy. Her nights were agony as she relived the way he had pleasured her in the tent, then fantasized all the other things they might do to one another if he came to her. Why hadn't she at least pleasured him the same way when she had had the chance?

In the darkest hours, when she was sweaty and aching with desire, she rose and walked to the closed door between their apartments but couldn't bring herself to knock.

Was he being honorable? Giving her time to adjust to their marriage as he had promised he would? Or had he completely lost interest in her?

She always went back to bed bereft, wondering what she had done to turn him off.

As brutal as the nights were, the days were far worse. Each time she was in his presence, she fought lust. His lips on the rim of a coffee cup made her shake with desire. His voice stroked across her skin, causing her pulse to race. If she caught his scent, she had to close her eyes and take control of herself.

Even now, anticipating being alone with him, her intimate regions were tingling with anticipation. Her one-track mind turned to fantasies of making love on the floor of his very closet, his naked weight upon her. His thick shaft piercing—

Flushed and impatient with herself, she went back into the main area.

The only thing worse than suffering this constant yearning would be his discovering how deeply she felt it and feeling nothing in return.

She shook herself out of her mental whirl by taking a more thorough look around the main room. Did he even come in here? There wasn't a speck of dust in sight, but she had the sense he spent very little time in here.

A sofa and chairs were arranged to face a television, should there be breaking news he needed to watch, but the cushions were undented. The liquor cabinet held nothing, not even nonalcoholic choices.

When she looked at the books, they were also dust free and arranged with precision, but who read actual books anymore? Especially dry nonfiction. Give her a romance and she would sneeze her way through the most yellowed pages, but biographies and history? No, thanks.

She couldn't help touching the mane of the gold lion that lounged on an ebony bookend. His one front paw was relaxed and dangling off the edge. His tail appeared about to swish. It was an eye-catching piece, one that looked vaguely familiar, making her think she'd seen something like it, perhaps by the same artist. She would have remembered if she'd seen this one. It was not only startlingly lifelike, with the animal's musculature lovingly recreated, it emanated power along with the innate playfulness of cats. The lion peered around the edge of the upright slab of ebony that he lounged against, as if waiting on his mate. Inviting her to come to his side of the books.

Galila looked for the match, but there was only

the one. Strange. Bookends came in pairs, didn't they? That was why there was an expression about things being "bookended."

She looked on the desk for it, then realized the heavy curtains behind the desk hid a pair of tall doors that led onto a balcony. She pulled them open.

Was this where his father had fallen?

She wasn't a morbid person, but something drew her to open the doors and step onto the shaded balcony. The heat crushed like a wall, but the view of the sea was stunning. There was a broader balcony on the other side of the palace that was used for ceremonies. It overlooked a public square and had been a means of addressing the masses before television.

This one, like the room behind her, was a place for reflection.

With an unforgiving courtyard a fatal distance below.

"No," Karim said, startling her into gasping and spinning. She clutched her chest where her heart leaped.

Mouth tight, Karim pointed her back into the center of the room.

"I didn't—I was just—"

He closed and locked the doors, then drew the drapes across with a yank on the cord. The room became cooler and darker, but she was still hot and flustered.

"Karim." She had come in here on a wave of temper, determined to confront him, but found herself in the middle of the carpet with her hands linked before her, apologies on her tongue.

"It's not up for discussion," he stated.

She didn't have to ask him if that was where the accident had happened. She could see the truth in his severe expression. He'd been six. How was it such a painful, visceral memory for him?

As she searched his expression, her infernal attraction to him began to take root and flourish through her. She noted how handsome he was in his business attire of pants and a button shirt. Nothing special, but it was tailored to his strong shoulders and framed his hips just so. He was as sexy and casually powerful as the lion she had admired.

He also had a thorn in his paw. She yearned to be the one who pulled it, she realized. The one he cherished for healing him.

"The ambassador and his wife will arrive soon. You should change."

It was a dismissal.

They were alone for the first time since the tent and he didn't have any use for her. Just like that, her temper flared. She remembered why she had been so infuriated, why she had hiked the distance across the massive palace to confront him.

"I need to talk to you." She folded her arms, chin set.

"It can't wait?"

"Until when? Do you propose I discuss my doctor's appointment over the dessert course so our guests can weigh in?"

His whole body tightened, as if bracing himself. His brows slammed together and his gaze swept her up and down. "What's wrong?"

"Nothing," she admitted, realizing she had

alarmed him, which was a tiny bit gratifying since he hadn't given her any indication of even a mild passing concern for her health and well-being since he'd poured out her brandy the night they met. "I mean, it's not a health problem, if that's what you're thinking."

He made an impatient noise and flicked his hand at her. "That's exactly what I thought. But if you're healthy, then what?"

"I want to know why you told the doctor I could go on whatever birth control I would prefer."

His head went back with surprise. "You said you didn't want children right away."

How was it possible for him to become *more* inscrutable? He pushed his fists into his pockets. The motion drew the fabric of his trousers tight across his fly, which revealed the hint of his masculine flesh.

She had been spending way too much time wondering about that part of him and her guilty conscience pushed heat into her cheeks. She forced herself not to stare and looked instead to the hardness in his jaw. Something in his stance made her think he'd been offended when she had told him she didn't have a particular desire to have his children, which had been true-ish at the time.

Now, she folded her arms, defensive because she was so—oh, she was going to have to own it. She was frustrated. Sexually.

"Aside from the fact it is not *your* decision what I put in *my* body," she declared hotly and for all womankind, "I don't understand why you think birth control is necessary when you seem to have decided on abstinence."

He blinked. His face relaxed with a hint of satisfaction that made her think of the lion swishing his tail, pleased he wouldn't have to run her to ground because she was edging close enough he wouldn't have to make any effort to chase her at all.

Oh, he read her agitation like it was a neon sign, she could tell. She blushed even harder.

"Hot and bothered, are you? We agreed to wait until after the wedding ceremony next week."

"Is that what we agreed? I thought you stated it

and I have been given no opportunity to discuss it. What happened to it being my choice what happened between us in bed?"

His eye ticked, then his jaw hardened.

"If you can't wait for our wedding night…" His hands came out of his pockets and he waved them slowly at himself in offering. "Help yourself."

As bluffs went, it almost worked. She was still a virgin and already feeling very scorned by him. This was daylight, not the safety of a pitch-black tent. Years of reading sexy romance novels, a rich fantasy life and curiosity were all a far cry from the reality of staring down a fully dressed man whose mouth was curling with smug knowledge that he was getting the better of her.

Because he thought she was some trembling wallflower who wouldn't make advances.

Well, he thought wrong. She was sick of feeling like his dalliance. A flame of fury glowed hot within her, refusing to be at the mercy of his whims. She would not be the only one obsessing about how they would feel together. *She* could give *him* pleasure.

She was determined to prove it.

When she walked up to him, however, and he loomed over her despite the heels she wore, her heart began to beat fast with apprehension. This was a dangerous game.

He didn't lower his head to cover her offered mouth. He made her set a hand behind his head and draw him down into *her* kiss. Then he had the gall not to respond to her first uncertain advances. *All* men wanted to kiss her. Didn't he realize that?

She forced her tongue between his lips and pressed harder, rocking her mouth under his as she pulled his tongue into her own mouth.

He made a growling, primal noise and encircled her with hard arms as he took over the kiss with passionate roughness. It lasted for a few uncontrolled, thrilling heartbeats before he caught her arms in a firm grip and set them apart from each other.

His gaze clashed into hers with accusation, as if she'd forced him to react in a way he didn't care for.

But that brief crack in his control only fueled her resolve. She brushed his hands off her arms and pressed his wrists behind his back, meeting his fierce glare with a scolding one.

"You just gave yourself to me, didn't you? Are you going back on that? What are you afraid of?"

Her breasts grazed his chest and their thighs brushed through the fabric of her skirt and his pants. She could feel he was aroused and that bolstered her confidence even more.

"I'm not afraid of anything." His voice was gritty, his words pushed through clenched teeth. "But what are you planning to do? Lose your virginity here on my desk?"

"I'm going to make love to you with my mouth," she dared to say, and felt the jolt that went through him. The muscled wrists in her hands became rock-hard, strained tendons as he bunched his hands into tight fists.

She smiled under a rush of feminine power.

"Do you like that idea?" She drew back a little and brought one hand to his fly. She caressed his

hard flesh through the fabric. "I think you do."
She did. Her hand was trembling.

His nostrils flared, but he held himself very
still. She couldn't tell if he was trying to act unaffected or if they were playing a game of chicken
and he was waiting for her to lose her nerve first.

She might. She'd never done anything so boldly
wicked.

With two shaking hands, she unbuttoned his
shirt and spread it wide, indulging herself by
splaying her hands across his hot skin and the
light sprinkle of hair. She turned her face back
and forth against the contours of his pecs, played
her touch over his rib cage before she licked at
his nipples to see if he reacted.

He did. He made a harsh noise and his fist went
into her hair, but he didn't force her to stop. When
she offered her mouth this time, he took it like
a starving man, without hesitation, greedy and
rapacious.

She almost lost herself to that kiss. Her blood
was running like wildfire, her oxygen all but
eaten up. She longed to let him take control, but

she also needed to prove to both of them that she wasn't alone in this sea of lust.

She ran her hands over his buttocks, then traced her fingers beneath the waistband of his pants until she came to the front.

She unbuckled and unzipped, stepped back enough to open his pants and push them down his hips. Then she eased the black line of his shorts down, exposing the thick flesh that had been keeping her up nights. Her breaths were coming in deep pants, like she'd been running for an hour, breasts rising and falling.

"You've taken this far enough," he said grimly, catching her hand before she touched him.

"You don't want me to?" She looked up at him with craving nearly blinding her.

Whatever he saw in her expression caused his own pupils to expand. The heat between them was like flames, licking back and forth, scorching. Shadows of struggle fought with a glaze of desperate hunger in his eyes.

"I want to," she assured him in a husky whisper, sinking to her knees before him.

She didn't know exactly what to do, but there didn't seem to be a wrong move as she lightly caressed and explored, getting to know his shape. Her first touch had him sucking in a breath. His flesh seemed to welcome her grasp with pulses of enjoyment. He muttered imprecations between ragged breaths, but didn't stop her.

He watched her with a fierce, avid gaze that only encouraged her to steady him for the first dab of her tongue.

Then he tipped back his head and groaned loudly at the ceiling, like it was pain and pleasure combined. She lost herself then, did everything she could to pleasure him with exactly as much devotion as he had shown her in the Bedouin tent. And when he was reaching the peak of his endurance, when his hand was in her hair and he was warning her he couldn't last, she was so aroused, she couldn't resist touching herself and finding release at the same time he did.

Karim left his stained, sweat-damp clothing on the floor of the closet and dressed in fresh

pants and a shirt, shaken and stunned—utterly
stunned—by what his wife had just done to him.

He came back into the main room and she
was already gone from the bathroom where she
had retreated moments after taking him to such
heights of ecstasy that he had thought he was
dying.

What a way to go.

He looked around the room he passionately
hated and knew his regard for it had been completely rewritten. He would always think of her
now, when he was in here. Galila on her knees
before him, hair a silk rope that bound both his
fists to the back of her head. Her mouth working
over his tip, her slender fingers a vice of pleasure
around his shaft. And then, when his fantasy-
turned-reality could not possibly have become
more erotic, she had burrowed her hand beneath
her skirt and pleasure had hummed in her throat
as they found satisfaction together.

How could any man withstand such a thing?

He ran his hand down his face, trying to put his
melted features into some semblance of control

before he had to rejoin his staff, let alone ambassadors from around the world.

He had been avoiding her, it was true. The more he wanted her, the more he fought against going to her. Making himself wait until their "wedding night" had seemed a suitable, if arbitrary way of proving he could control his lust and resist her.

Like hell. He had lost the battle the second he'd been told she was waiting for him, never mind when she had sidled up to him and kissed him.

This had been a defeat, one he already regretted, even as his blood purred in his veins and every bit of tension in his body had left him.

With regret, he squatted and swept his hand across the nap of the carpet, erasing where his own footprints faced the impression of her knees.

As he squatted there, from this vantage, he was the height he had been when his father had sat at that desk, rambling about things Karim hadn't even comprehended.

I love her. Do you understand? Your mother can never know. She doesn't know. Doesn't understand what this kind of love is like. Pray you never experience it, my son. It destroys your soul. And now she says it's over. How do I go on? I can't. Do you understand, Karim? I cannot live without her. I'm sorry, but I can't.

Karim hadn't understood. But the memory was a timely reminder as to why he had been trying to avoid giving in to his desire for Galila. Such intense passion could very easily become addictive. Obsessive and soul-destroying.

As he straightened, he pulled on the cloak of control he'd been wearing since bringing her here, determined to set her at a distance and keep her there. Permanently this time.

It wasn't easy. An hour later, she arrived at his side wearing a hijab, since the ambassador and his wife were Muslim. Somehow her conservative gown and face framed in closely draped indigo were more provocative than one of her knee-length skirts with a fitted jacket.

Galila was beautiful no matter what she wore, but he could barely keep his gaze off the lips that had left a stain of pink on his flesh, or the lashes that had framed the wide eyes that had looked up at him.

He quickly made a remark about a political situation and drew the ambassador aside so he wouldn't embarrass himself by becoming freshly aroused.

This constant flow of dinners and entertaining had been partly a series of prescheduled meetings, but also a necessary means of introducing his wife to key dignitaries before the celebration that would cement her as his wife and queen. Their marriage had been surprise enough. With all the rumblings of concern at lower levels, he had to ensure she was accepted.

Galila, he had to acknowledge, had a particular gift for charming people onto her side. She flowed effortlessly from small talk over the best shoe designer in Milan to a policy discussion. If she had a question, she asked it in a way that never seemed impertinent. If she had an opinion, she always managed to voice it in a way that was nonconfrontational but made her point.

As for the reports he received daily on the various decisions she was making as queen, well, he was grateful to have fewer things to worry about so he could concentrate on the ones that had broader impact.

"Oh, you know my father?" she asked with surprise now, voice drawing Karim back to the dinner and the conversation.

"That's an overstatement," the ambassador said with an embarrassed wave of his hand. "I met him, well, it must have been thirty years ago? I was quite young, just starting my first career as a translator. He came to our country as part of a diplomatic tour. He has such a sharp mind. I very much admired him and only wanted to express my concern for his health, given he stepped aside recently. I hope he's well?"

"Grieving my mother." Galila stiffened slightly, just enough for Karim to notice, but this was another area where she seemed to finesse her way without a misstep.

"I expect he was quite heartbroken. I'm sure you all are, but, well, it was obvious to me, even back then, how much he loved her. He cut short his tour to be with her. I remember it so clearly because I couldn't imagine having a woman in my life whom I couldn't bear to be apart from. Then I met one." He smiled at his wife.

She blushed and told him not to embarrass them.

Galila offered a smile, but it didn't reach her eyes. She stared off into the middle distance a moment, murmuring, "I didn't realize he had ever been apart from her for any length of time. It certainly never happened in my memory, but that would have been before I was born."

If she did the math and realized Karim's father had killed himself roughly thirty years ago...

"We need to add a discussion on your country's foreign banking regulations to tomorrow's agenda," Karim cut in, changing the subject.

Moments later, the women had moved on to an innocuous topic and the rest of the evening passed without incident. He realized, however, that this was another angle of vulnerability he had to protect himself against. His marriage of expedience was a minefield of potential disaster.

* * *

Galila excused herself the moment their guests were gone. She had a lot to think about. Deep down, she was still reeling from her experience with Karim, feeling self-conscious about the way she had behaved.

When she saw him at dinner with the ambassador, he had once again been the remote man who revealed only the barest hint of regard toward her. His indifference crushed her soul into the dust, but she hadn't allowed herself to look him in the eye or her gaze to linger on his expression. She had fought all evening to hide her aching soul, asking mindless questions and pretending an interest in the wife's dog-breeding techniques.

Then the ambassador had made that remark about her father's trip thirty years ago.

She had enough going on with her new marriage that she shouldn't have room for obsessing over her mother's lover, but she couldn't help but wonder. She couldn't ask her father about his trip, but she sent an email to both her brothers, keeping her inquiry very vague, asking if they knew anything about that particular trip their father had taken. She doubted they would. Malak hadn't been born and Zufar had been a toddler.

Still, she sighed with disappointment when she received their blunt "No" replies the next morning.

"What's wrong?" Karim asked as he nodded to accept more coffee.

"Nothing. I asked my brothers if they knew anything about that diplomatic tour my father went on, the one the ambassador mentioned. They don't."

"Why?"

She looked at him, conveying with a flick of her lashes that it probably wasn't a topic that should be raised in front of the servants. "I'm curious about it."

He knew exactly what she was telegraphing and said dismissively, "I don't see that it matters."

"With all due respect," she said in a carefully level tone, "it wouldn't seem important to you because it doesn't concern your parent. I have questions, however."

The listening ears would think she was still talking about her father, but she meant her mother and Adir. Perhaps Karim took offense at her remark despite her attempt to maintain a suitable amount of deference. His fingers tightened on the handle of his coffee mug.

"Surely you have more important things to do with your time. How are the reception plans coming?"

She knew when she was being patronized and flipped her hair. "Perfectly. Your excellent staff would provide nothing less." She smiled at the hovering assistants.

The party was only days away, and much as she enjoyed being the center of attention, she was quite nervous. Everything would be exquisite, she had no doubt at all, but Karim intended for them to consummate their marriage that night and she was having mixed feelings about that.

She had wanted to prove something to him yesterday, but she wasn't sure what. That she was brave? That she would be a lover who would satisfy him? That he couldn't resist her?

What she had discovered was that even when she took the initiative, she had no control over her reaction. No modesty or inhibition.

In fact, the more she thought about their encounter, the more anxious she became. She kept seeing herself as besotted as her father was with her mother. Loyal as a hound, he'd loved his spouse into her death despite the fact she had committed adultery and never gave more than passing consideration to the children she had made with him.

Even more of a fearful thought was that she might become as dependent on Karim's regard as she had been on her mother's. For a time, she might be his sexual pet. There was a certain novelty within a new marriage, she was sure. They might both indulge themselves, but he had already demonstrated that his desire was fickle. He could turn his emotions on and off on a whim.

She couldn't bear to invest herself in him, grow to care for him, only to have that rug pulled. How would she withstand years of his casual indifference?

At least as a daughter, she'd been able to escape to Europe and distract herself with schooling. But charity work and its accompanying accolades only went so far in filling up the void inside her. She needed more.

Karim, however, would never offer the "more" she sought.

Why? What was wrong with her? What was her great flaw? She had convinced herself that her mother's fading beauty had caused her to grow jealous as Galila's allure ripened, but Karim was behaving with the same ambivalence toward her.

Perhaps that meant there was a deeper shortcoming inside her that kept people from truly loving her?

She was a kind person, an obedient daughter. She was trying to be a loyal wife, but Karim didn't even seem to value that much in her. It was agonizing.

She had no choice as far as attending the reception went, but she didn't know if she could become his wife in every sense of the word afterward. He would surely break her heart.

CHAPTER SIX

CORONATIONS WERE NOT a lavish affair in this part of the world. Galila knew that from her own country and had been told that Karim had a cousin appointed as his successor should he fail to produce one. That designation and the allegiance of all his cousins and other dignitaries had been handled with public, verbal pledges witnessed by the rest.

Recognizing Galila as his queen had been a matter of Karim stating that he had chosen her that night in the Bedouin encampment. It was all the people of Zyria had needed to accept and recognize her as their monarch, but they would feel cheated of a party if he didn't host one.

That was all that this day was—a formal celebration here in the palace, but one followed by all. Festivities were extended across the country, providing the entire population a reason to take a day to enjoy themselves.

Galila was nothing if not scrupulously adept at planning this sort of event. Along with charity work abroad and at home, she had always led the charge on family events—to a point. Her mother had liked Galila to do all the work of choosing menus and decor, then always swooped in at the last minute to change the color scheme or the order of the speeches, putting her own stamp on it.

This time, every single detail was Galila's own.

As part of that, she had carefully considered the message the event would send. Obviously, she had to convey that she was pleased to be Karim's wife and that she embraced her new country. She needed to highlight the advantage of a union with Khalia, too. It was a celebration and needed to be lavish enough to reflect their position, but she didn't want to pin *spendthrift* to her lapel and require years to remove it. She wanted it known that she was eager to begin charity work, but didn't want to appear critical and suggest Zyria was failing to meet the needs of its people.

The guest list had been its own Gordian knot to unravel and there had also been kosher meals and other diverse religious observances that had to be considered.

In the end, Galila pulled a small cheat by adding some well-respected professionals to the mix. She seated doctors and teachers next to ministers and other dignitaries with appropriate portfolios. Everything in the swag bags from silk scarves to gold bangles to a jar of spices had been sourced in Zyria, showcasing their best merchants.

Within the speeches, she had the treasury minister praise her for being under budget with this party. He announced that she had asked for the savings to be donated to a traveling medical unit that would service some of the most difficult to access places in Zyria. It was met with an appropriate round of appreciative applause.

Her husband promptly upstaged her by announcing that a hospital wing to service women's health issues would be built in her name. Her reaction must have been priceless because everyone laughed and applauded even harder while she covered her hot cheeks with her hands.

It was a political gesture, she reminded herself. A means of ensuring she was accepted and welcomed and cemented into Zyria's history books.

She was still touched by the gesture, perhaps because he looked at her with sincere regard as he said, "I'm hoping you'll take an active role in this project. Your instincts and attention to detail are excellent."

"Did you mean that?" she asked as he seated himself next to her again.

"Of course." He seemed surprised by her question. "I've been kept apprised of every decision you've made here so far."

That was news. She had been quite convinced he hadn't thought of her more than twice since they'd met.

"You've done an excellent job," he said, sounding sincere. His gaze skimmed across the four hundred people dressed to the nines, jewelry sparkling and gold cutlery flashing as they dined on their first course beneath faux starlight. Land-marks were projected onto the walls beneath swathes of fabric to resemble looking out from a Bedouin tent on Zyria's landscape. The center-pieces were keepsake lanterns amid Zyrian flora and the scent of Zyrian incense hung on the air.

"I don't know that anyone will dare eat these chocolates, but they will certainly enjoy show-ing them off. Very ingenious." He tilted the treat that decorated each place setting. It was made of camel milk by a Zyrian chocolatier and shaped like Zyria and Khalia stuck together as one piece, the border only a subtle shift in color, not a di-viding line. She had prevailed on her brother to send coffee and cinnamon from Khalia to flavor their side of it while the Zyrian was spiced with nutmeg and cardamom.

"It's a subtle yet brilliant touch."

Brilliant?

Don't be needy.

But she was. In her core, she was starved for validation. Which was exactly the problem with this marriage. She wanted—needed—to believe

Karim valued her. That whatever he felt toward her was real and permanent.

He was in demand at all times, however. It was somewhat understandable that after his brief compliment, his attention went elsewhere. They didn't speak again until the plates had been cleared and they moved to the adjoining ballroom to begin the dancing.

Here she'd been a little freer with the Western influences, bringing in colored lights and a DJ who played current pop tunes from around the globe, but included many of the hits by Arab bands.

Their first dance was an older ballad, however, one Karim's mother had told her had been played at her wedding to Karim's father. It was meant as a reassurance to the older generation that things were changing but only a little.

Karim wore his ceremonial robes and she was in several layers of embroidered silk over a brocade gown with jewels in her hair, at her wrists, around her neck and even a bejeweled broach worn on a wide band around her middle.

Karim had to be very careful as he took her into his arms. He muttered something under his breath about hugging a cactus.

"I understood it to be an heirloom that all Zyrian queens wear on special occasions," she said, affected by his closeness despite the fact he had to maintain enough distance not to catch his robes on the piece.

"My staff was too shy to explain it was designed as a chastity belt, worn when the king was not around to protect his interests."

"Talk about putting a ring on it," she said under her breath.

He snorted, the sound of amusement so surprising, she flashed a look upward in time to see the corner of his mouth twitch.

"Yes, well, the king is in the house so we'll dispense with it as soon as possible."

Her heart swerved in the crazy jitter of alarm and anticipation she'd been suffering as this day drew nearer. It was so silly! They were familiar with each other. She knew she would find pleasure with him.

But what happened after that? Would he go back to ignoring her? She wouldn't be able to stand it. How could she give herself to a man who would only rebuff her afterward?

Karim stole her away to her apartment as soon as he could, dismissing the staff that hovered to help undress her. He could handle that himself, thank you very much.

On his instruction, the rooms had been prepared with a fresh bath, rose petals, candles, cordial and exotic fruits. The music of gently plucked strings played quietly in the background. Silk pajamas had been left on the bed for both of them—and would be swept to the floor unused if he had his way.

Alone with his wife for the first time since she'd blown his mind in his library the other day, he was fairly coming out of his skin with anticipation—not that he would admit to it. Oh, he knew damned well that part of him had been counting the minutes until he could release himself from his self-imposed restraint, but he barely acknowledged that. It was pure weakness to feel this way, damn it, but he couldn't put off consummation forever.

In fact, he had begun to rationalize that the reason he was growing obsessive about the moment of possession was merely because he hadn't yet done so. Once they made love, he wouldn't be so preoccupied by how delicious it might be.

That was the only reason urgency gripped him and put a gruff edge on his voice when he commanded her to turn around. "Let me relieve you of that thing."

She jolted a bit and didn't meet his eyes as she turned so he could remove the elaborate belt.

Her spine grew taller as he released the dozen tiny hook-and-eye fasteners. She drew a deep breath as he set it aside, then, when he touched her shoulders to remove her outer robe, she stiffened again and glanced warily over her shoulder.

He hesitated, but she shrugged to help him peel it away. It was surprisingly heavy with its detailed embroidery locking in pearls and other jewels. If anything, her tension grew as he eased it away, however.

She turned and folded her arms, now in a strapless gown bedecked with a band of silver and diamonds beneath the extravagant necklace that had been his wedding gift to her. She pressed her lips together, conveying wary uncertainty.

"What's wrong?"

"Nothing," she said a little too quickly, shoulders coming up in a shrug and staying in a defensive hunch.

He moved closer and had to tilt her chin up, then wait for her gaze to come to his. A tiny flinch plucked at her brows and her gaze swept away, anxious to avoid his.

"Galila," he murmured. "Are you being shy?" It seemed impossible, considering the intimacies they'd shared, but her mouth twitched.

She hitched a shoulder, nodding a little, lashes dropping to hide her gaze again.

"There's no rush," he assured her, even though it felt like a lie. Standing this close to her, feeling the softness of her cheek under the caress of his thumb, he didn't know how he had managed to wait this long. The starving beast inside him was waking and stretching, prowling in readiness to go on the hunt.

When he started to lower his mouth to hers, she stiffened with subtle resistance.

He drew back, experiencing something like alarm. Was she teasing him on purpose?

"I'm nervous, it's fine," she insisted, but she was still avoiding his gaze.

Her crown had been fitted with a silver and blue veil that draped over the rich, loose waves of her hair. She reached to remove it.

"I'll do it." He searched out the pins that secured it, distantly thinking he should have delegated this task to the one who'd put them in. It was an intricate process and she winced a couple of times, even though he was as gentle as he could be.

He persevered and finally was able to leave the crown and veil on a table. She ran her fingers through her hair—an erotic gesture at the best of times. Tonight, she was especially entrancing.

The smooth swells of her breasts lifted against the blue velvet. Her heavily decorated ivory skirt shimmered, merely hinting at the lissome limbs it hid.

"You're so beautiful, it almost hurts the eyes." The words came from a place he barely acknowledged within himself, one where his desire for her was a craven thing that he could barely contain.

She dropped her hands in front of her. "I can't help the way I look."

"It's not a drawback," he said drily, moving to take up her hands and set them on his shoulders. His own then went to her rib cage, finding her supple as a dancer. Her heels put her at exactly the most comfortable height to dip his head and capture her mouth with his own.

A jolt of electricity seemed to jump between them, reassuring him even as his mouth stung and she made a sound of near pain. He quickly assuaged the sensation with a full, openmouthed kiss. The kind he'd been starving for. The kind that should have slaked something in him, but only stoked his hunger.

She began to melt into him and he felt mind-lessness begin to overtake him, the same loss of control that had pinned him in place while she stole every last shred of his discipline that day in his library.

He tightened his hands on her and started to set her back a step, needing to keep a clear head.

She made a noise of hurt and the heels of her hands exerted pressure, urging him to release her altogether.

His reflexes very nearly yanked her back in close. Some primitive refusal to be denied was that close to overwhelming him.

The push-pull was startling enough to freeze him with his hands still keeping her before him, so he could read her face.

"Do you not want—?" He had to look away, not ready to hear that she was rejecting him.

"I do, but—"

She did break from his hold then, brushing his

hands off her and pacing away a few steps. The action raked something cold across him.

She turned back to hold out a beseeching hand. "I can't bear the games, Karim."

She looked stricken enough to cause a sharp sensation to pierce his heart.

"Make love to me if you want to. But don't... Don't tell me I'm beautiful, then act like you can't stand how I look. Don't kiss me like you can't get enough, then push me away as though I'm someone you dislike. Don't tell a roomful of people that you think I'm wonderful when you clearly think I'm not. I can't go through those ups and downs again. I can't."

He narrowed his eyes. "What are you talking about? I don't dislike you."

She closed her eyes. "It doesn't matter how you feel, just be honest about it. And consistent. Please. It's fine that you only want me a little, the way any man might respond to any available woman. Don't pander to me and act like..."

"What?" he prompted, bracing because he was afraid that he might have betrayed too much somewhere along the line. Definitely when she'd taken him in her mouth.

"I don't know," she said with a break in her voice. "I don't know how you feel. That's the issue. Sometimes you act as though you like me, but then...you don't."

"Of course, I like you, Galila." He swallowed, thinking he understood the issue here. In a gentler tone, he added, "But I told you in the beginning not to expect love from me."

"I'm not talking about love, Karim! I'm talking about basic regard. You've barely spoken to me since the day in your office. You act like it didn't even happen! Then you think saying a few nice things tonight—that I'm so beautiful you can't stand to look at me—and think that makes me want to..." She waved at the bed, then her arm dropped in defeat.

His heart skewed in his chest. "That's not the way I meant it, Galila."

"The worst part is, I still want to have sex with you. But be honest about how it will be afterward. If you're only going to ignore me until the next time an urge strikes, then don't arrange rose petals and candles and act like you want me to *feel* something tonight. Don't act like this is a special moment for either one of us. Not when you're only going to pretend I don't exist afterward."

He pinched the bridge of his nose. This was special. It was her first time. Did she think he didn't have some nerves about that? The responsibility to *make* it special?

"I wanted you to relax."

"Well, I can't." She shook off whatever melancholy was in her expression and reached to remove her earrings. "Let's just get it done so you can lock yourself back in your room."

"Get it done?" he repeated as a sick knot tightened in his gut. "I want our lovemaking to be a pleasure for you, Galila. Not a chore."

"I'm not like you! When we…do things, I feel it. Emotionally." She pressed her curled hand between her breasts. "And you're manipulating me with that. Maybe not on purpose. Maybe you don't even realize how badly you're knocking my feelings around, but you are. I can't do that for a night, Karim, let alone a lifetime. I accept that this is an arranged marriage, not one based on love. But don't act like you care and then prove that you don't. I can't bear that. Not again."

If she had plunged a knife into his lung, she wouldn't have winded him this badly. Her accusations were bad enough, but suddenly he was wondering if she had given her heart to another and been rejected. And if she had, why was he taking that far worse than he would have if she'd had other lovers physically?

"Who else did that to you?" He needed to know.

"It doesn't matter," she muttered, turning away to work bangles off her wrists.

"It's affecting our marriage. Our relationship." What the hell did he care about such things? She was handing him a free pass to make love to her and withhold any investment of deeper feelings. He ought to rejoice. Instead, he was aggrieved by the idea of her coming to their marriage bed withholding anything from him, especially the genuine excitement and delight she had seemed to take in their congress before.

Running a hand over his head, he demanded, "Who?"

She sighed and stayed silent a long time, while her jewelry went into a dish with soft clinks.

"In light of what we've learned about my mother recently," she began in a subdued voice, "I understand better why she was so ambivalent with my brothers. Why she pushed them away. She had given away a child she wanted to keep. That has to break something in you. Maybe that's even why she eventually pushed me away, but it wasn't always like that. For years…"

Her shoulders slumped under an invisible weight.

"None of this really matters, Karim," she said faintly.

His ardor was well and truly doused. Short of an invasion that required him to protect his country, he could not imagine anything more important to him than what she was telling him right now.

"Continue," he commanded.

"It makes me sound very pathetic. As superficial as you think I am." She kept her back to him and spoke to her feet. "When I was a child, I felt very special. It was obvious to me that I was the one Mother loved. Father worshipped her and she gave him nothing. The boys learned to live without affection from her, but she adored me. She brushed my hair and dressed me so we looked alike. She took me everywhere with her and was always so proud and happy when people said I was pretty and looked like her."

"That makes you sound more like a pet than her child."

"I was. A living doll, maybe. If only I had stayed that way."

"What way? Young?"

"Preadolescent, yes. Once I started to become a woman, it stopped."

"What did?"

"Her love."

She clutched her elbows in clawlike fingers, manicured nails threatening to cut into the skin of her bare arms. He moved across to touch her, drawing her attention to it so she would stop hurting herself.

She gave a little shiver and flashed a distressed glance up to him, then stepped away, averting her face.

"How do you know she stopped loving you? What happened?"

"Instead of saying, *You're so beautiful*, she would say, 'Your perfume has soured.' Instead of saying, *I love how your smile is exactly like mine*, she would say, 'Your laugh is too high-pitched. That lipstick is not your color.'"

"Did you do something to anger her?"

"If I did, she never said outright what it was." Her tone grew bitter.

"Then why do you think—? Ah. You told me before that she didn't want to be called Grandmother," he recalled.

"She said those exact words one time when my father was telling me over a family dinner that I ought to marry."

"So she was jealous of your youth."

"Maybe even that my life was ahead of me.

I've been thinking about her all day today, thinking she would have died rather than attend *my* wedding. She hated it when I was the center of attention and would always say, 'You're acting like Malak.' She really did hate him and wasn't afraid to show it."

Galila had never acknowledged that out loud, but it felt weirdly good to do so. Like lancing a wound so it could begin to heal.

"And now you have no opportunity to ask her about it. I do understand that frustration, you know."

She sent him a helpless look, one palm coming up.

"You see? You're doing it again. Making it seem like we have something in common, that you care what I might have been through. What happens in ten minutes, though? In an hour? In the morning? Will my feelings become inconsequential again?"

He looked away from her, uncomfortable as he viewed his behavior in a fresh light. He had been protecting himself—his whole country, he could argue—since Zyria had been impacted when his father threw his life away over a broken heart. But he hadn't seen that in protecting himself, he had been injuring her.

"Is it me, Karim?" she asked in a voice thick with dread. "I had nearly convinced myself that my mother's hurtful behavior was her own issue, but if you're doing the same thing, then there must be a flaw in *me*." Her voice cracked as she pointed at her breastbone. "Something that makes me impossible to love. What is it?"

Galila stood in a vice of agony while her husband stood unmoving, as a man made from marble. She didn't even think he breathed. Was he trying to spare her? Because he was alleviating none of her fears with that stoic expression.

Finally, he blinked and muttered, "There's nothing wrong with you. That's absurd."

"There you go. I'm absurd!" She felt exactly as she had in those first dark years when her mother had begun to pull away. "I know I'm a ridiculous person. My brothers told me all the time that I shouldn't be so needy and want to feel loved. I know that with some people, like you, there's no getting into their good graces, even when you once were loved by them. But I don't understand how I *lose* it. Is it things that I say? Am I supposed to stand in silence and allow myself to be admired? But why would anyone want to look at me? I'm not beautiful *enough*. My neck is too long and I have my mother's thighs. Is it because my nose is too pointy? Help me understand, Karim! I can't fix it if I don't know what the problem is."

"There is no problem," he said so firmly she could only take it as a knife in the heart because he clearly wasn't going to tell her.

She threw up her hands in defeat. "Fine. Let's just—" She waved at the bed, but tears came into her eyes. She didn't know if she could go through with it. All she could do was stand there, crushed by anguish, fighting not to break down.

"Galila. There is nothing wrong with you," he insisted, coming across to take her hands. "Look at me." He dipped his head and waited until she was looking into his eyes. "You're very engaging. Very easy to…"

His mouth tightened and she could see him pulling himself back behind some invisible wall.

She tried to pull away, but he tightened his grip on her hands.

"Listen. I find myself letting down my guard with you. That's not something I ever do. Not with anyone except perhaps my mother. Even then…it's not comfortable for me."

"Well, it's not comfortable for me to let down my guard only to be shut out afterward. That's why I'm still a virgin. That sort of intimacy isn't easy for me, either. Not unless I'm convinced my heart will be safe." She pulled her hands free and quarter-turned away. "Maybe that's what all relationships are, though? Maybe I am a fool, thinking there's some way to feel safe in one." She spun back. "But your mother and father were in love. It's possible, Karim."

He was the one to walk away this time, hand drawing down his face as he let out a harsh breath.

"I know what you're thinking," she said with despair frosting her insides. "That I'm ruining our honeymoon night. I don't mean to set ridiculous standards. I just…" *Find it all very disappointing. Heartbreakingly empty.* "I don't know how I'll live in this state of hurt for the rest of my life. How do you not care, then? Teach me *that*, Karim."

His shoulders flexed as though her words had struck like a whip across them. He shook his head, voice disembodied when he spoke.

"I have trained myself not to care, Galila. To keep my thoughts to myself and control my desires. A man in my position can't give in to urges and open up doorways to vulnerability. I can't, Galila. The kingdom depends on my strength." He turned to deliver that bad news in a voice that was calm and factual but kind, at least.

Her mouth trembled and she nodded. "I know. Look at my father, abdicating because he was so devastated by losing my mother, even after what she had done. I just don't know how to be like you, Karim, instead of like him."

"I don't want you to be like me," he said in a voice that was low and quiet, but carried an impact that seemed to go through her as a shock wave, shivering all her pieces into new alignments. "I like who you are, Galila."

"You don't even know me, Karim." Her eyes were hot, and she wanted so badly to believe him.

"Untrue. Look at this party tonight. It was a ridiculous expense, one where you could have made it all about yourself. Instead, you gave it meaning. You *are* beautiful, so beautiful you trick the mind into thinking that's all you are. Then you display intelligence and kindness and you navigate all aspects of my life—a life I fight to control every minute of every day—you walk through that obstacle course with a graceful lack of effort. It's astonishing to me how well you fit in."

"My mother should get the credit for preparing me for this life, not me," she pointed out, throat abraded by emotion.

"And humble on top of the rest."

"Karim, it's very nice of you to say these things, but—"

"I don't do platitudes, Galila," he cut in flatly. "I'm telling you what I have learned of you during our short union. You have qualities I didn't expect, but I never expected to have a partner at all. A wife, yes, but not someone who is a genuine support. It's the strangest thing to me. Do you understand that? I don't want to grow accustomed to your presence at my side. I never needed you before. Why should I need you now? But there it is. You make it easier to carry out my duties, even as I feel weak for allowing you to lift any of the load. It's a paradox I haven't worked out how to solve."

She was soaking up the mud with the rainwater, feeling the contradiction inside her while watching the dismay battle with resignation in his brutally handsome features.

"Do you understand that it's your reluctance to allow me to share in your life that is killing me? Every time you push me away and act like I'm more annoyance than necessity, I hurt. How do I relax and give myself to you tonight, then face your withdrawal tomorrow? When you've decided I've seen too much of you?"

His cheek ticked.

"I'm sorry," she whispered, shaking her head in defeat. "I don't think I can—"

"I won't," he cut in, tone thin and sharp as a dagger, one corner of his mouth pulling down into the deadly curve of a *jambiya* blade. He was tensile steel, pupils expanding and contracting with inner conflict—a warrior on the defensive, but ready and willing to attack.

"Won't...?"

"Shut you out. I won't," he vowed.

She searched his expression, anguished by the struggle she could see in him, disheartened by how clearly it went against the grain for him. "That's not a promise you want to make. I can see that much, Karim."

Why didn't he want to share himself with her?

His lips pulled back against his teeth.

"But I will." He came across to cup her cheek. His gaze dropped to her throat, where her pulse throbbed fast. His palm slid down to cover it, so her heartbeat was hitting the heel of his hand. "Because I would do almost anything to touch you." His voice was both graveled and velvety. "That is the crux of it. And I can't believe I am handing you that weapon."

He looked tortured, but if his statement was a weapon, it was one that disarmed her as thoroughly as him. Her eyes burned and the rest of her grew weak. With her own tentative trust building, she set her hand on his chest, where his heart hammered in fierce pounds that made her own echo in her ears.

"It's the same for me. You know it is," she whispered.

"Our souls may be destined for hell then, because I have tried to resist—"

He dipped his head and this time, when he dragged his mouth across hers, she melted. The harsh truth was, she wanted him far more than she feared the detriment he might become to her well-being.

And how could she deny the hunger in his

kiss? He was so unabashed it was as if he'd let himself off leash. His lips demanded while his tongue took and gave, making her whole body feel gripped in a force that was both energizing and weakening. The pulse that had raced in her throat grew to something she felt in the pit of her belly and at the juncture of her thighs. It was nervous anticipation. Knowledge that *this was it*.

Neither of them could be torn from the other now.

She clung to him, growing so hot, she whimpered in frustration because she didn't want to let him go to remove the rest of her clothing. Her one hand went to her back and tried to work the zipper.

He lifted his head, eyes glowing and avid, cheeks flushed, mouth wet and pulling in a nearly cruel grimace.

"We have time," he said roughly.

"I don't feel like we do," she said breathlessly, feeling overcome and anxious and—

With a feral noise, he scooped her up and strode

to the bed. His angular features were warrior sharp, hawkish and fierce.

"This," he said as he set her on the mattress and leaned on the hands he braced beside her shoulders. "This is what scares the hell out of me. It's your first time and I feel like an animal. If I don't control it, who will, Galila?"

"Come here," she demanded. Begged. And set her hand behind his head, moaning in tortured joy when his weight came down on her along with the heat of his lips against hers.

They attacked each other with erotic passion, legs tangling in her gown as she tried to make space for him. Her fingers caught at the collar of his robe, pulling at it so she could taste his shoulder when he dragged his tongue down the side of her neck. Somehow her teeth set against his skin and she had to restrain herself from biting down, but she wanted so ferociously to mark him, it was a fight to keep herself to a scrape and a threat of pain.

"Go ahead," he said, lifting his head and revealing a dark smile that was so transfixing, she felt it like the sun hitting her bare skin. It lit her up inside and out, nearly blinding her. "Claw at me. Bite me. I want all of it. Whatever is inside you."

She dragged her nails down his back through his robe, then dug them into his buttocks, hard as steel but flexing at her touch to drive his firm flesh against her sensitive mound.

He cupped her head and held her still for another rapacious kiss. Again and again, he feasted on her, satisfying yet stoking. Driving them both wild until she was ready to cry, she was in a state of such heightened arousal.

"I need to feel you," she panted when his hot mouth went down her throat again. "Please, Karim."

His answer was to yank at her bodice, baring her breast to his greedy mouth. She arched, crying out at the sharp pull on her nipple.

"Too hard?" His breath bathed her skin in a tease.

"Never," she gasped, and dragged at his robe, trying to get beneath it.

He shifted, went after her other nipple with equal fervor while he began gathering her gown up her thighs. The second he found skin, his hand climbed unerringly to the lace that shielded her most intimate flesh.

He groaned as he traced over it. She whimpered at the caress that was desperately needed and not nearly enough.

"Karim," she begged.

"So ready for me." He rose to kiss her, but his hand stayed beneath her gown. "Do you think about that night my mouth was here? I do. All the time."

His finger slid beneath the silk, parting and caressing, making speech impossible.

"I think about you in my office, touching yourself as you pleasured me. I'm jealous." He probed gently, licking at her panting mouth as he carefully penetrated. "I think about being here like this with you, having you in every way possible because I want you to be *mine*."

"I am," she swore, opening her legs to invite his touch deeper.

"I take care of what's mine." He pushed the silk firmly aside, his thick finger making love to her while his thumb teased the knot of nerves that made her writhe in pleasure.

She was going to die, held by his caress on a molten ledge, teased and stroked, heat building until that was all she was. Heat. Blistering heat. She bit her lip, wanting the release but fighting it.

"Karim," she managed to breathe, stilling his hand. "I want to feel you. Do this together."

His cheekbones were sharp above cheeks drawn taut. All of him was tense and flexed. Even his lips were pulled back from his teeth in effort.

"Yes," he hissed and very, very carefully withdrew, then he began to tug at her gown.

It took forever. They kept stopping to kiss. To groan. To caress bared skin and whisper, "Oh, yes. You smell so good. You're so smooth here. So lovely. So strong."

Somehow, they managed to strip and she made a keening noise in her throat as they rolled together. The aching swells of her breasts flattened by his hard chest, the roughness of his thighs abrading the insides of hers was sheer magic. She hadn't known that being naked, skin to skin, sex to sex would make her so weak. She hadn't known that his muscles and overwhelming size could be its own aphrodisiac, making her writhe in ecstasy simply because he was against her.

"Galila." His voice was an abrasive husk, savaged by the same limits of arousal that gripped her.

"I'm ready." She was going to weep. She was so achingly ready.

He slid against her, parting her folds, lined up for entry. And kissed her as he held himself there. He kissed her as though she was the most precious thing he had ever seen.

"No one else will ever give you this," he vowed against her mouth, brutally possessive, but truer words had never been spoken.

"No one could."

There was pressure, invasion. She stiffened a little in surprise, anticipating pain, bracing for it, but he kissed her so tenderly as he exerted that steady pressure.

For one second, as his implacable demand
threatened pain, she thought, *I can't*. Then it was
done and he seemed to become a part of her,
mouth open over her trembling lips, thumb caressing her cheek. His hard shape inside her was
strange, yet deeply wonderful.

"No one else will ever give me that," he said
with awe and pride. He nibbled her jaw, brushed
his lips at her temple, then kissed her once, very
sweetly. Then again, this time with more purpose. When he came back a third time, she clung
to his mouth with her own.

Their bodies shifted. There was tenderness
where they were joined, but nothing more than
she could handle, not when arousal was returning
with inescapable tingles and clenches of desire.

He was right. This was a type of pleasure she
couldn't give herself, couldn't have even imagined. She rubbed her face against his neck,
wallowing in the weight of his hips, the way
smoothing her inner thighs against his hips made
him groan.

When he began to withdraw, she clung on with

everything in her and he returned with a rush of sensation so acute she gasped.

"Oh," she breathed, beginning to understand.

"Yes," he said tightly, eyes deep pools, atavistic and regressive, yet he never lost control. He kept his pace slow, letting her get used to the feel of him forging his way, holding her well inside the concentric circles of pleasure that rang through her with each thrust.

She couldn't bear it, it was so good, and she turned her mouth against his iron-hard biceps, biting him. Only then did he make a primal noise and pick up the pace. The intensity redoubled. Her body undulated to receive him. The struggle to reach the pinnacle became a fight they fought together with ragged breaths and fisted hands and every ounce of strength they both possessed.

Then she was there, right there, the cataclysm a breath away. She locked her heels at the small of his back, determined to keep him inside her forever. At least while the waves of pleasure rolled over her.

He pressed deep, holding himself flush against her as culmination arrived.

They clung then, holding on to each other as the acute tension released in a near painful rush of heat and such encompassing waves of pleasure she could hardly breathe. If her eyes were open, she was blind. If he said things, she only heard the rush of blood in her ears. What happened to him happened to her, stopping time and holding her transfixed. They were one in a way she hadn't known was possible.

It was utter perfection that couldn't be maintained forever, which was a tragedy, she decided, as the rush subsided and the pulses began to fade and she discovered tears on her cheeks.

That supreme ecstasy could be replicated, however. They pleasured each other into delirium twice more before she fell asleep, bound to him in a way that could never be undone.

Which made waking to an empty bed that much more excruciating.

He had promised not to rebuff her, but here she was, forsaken, abandoned and alone. Again.

CHAPTER SEVEN

KARIM HAD MADE a terrible mistake. He had known it as he was offering a vow to Galila that put fissures in his defenses against her. He had known it as he chose to make that vow rather than put off consummation of their marriage—which would have proven his mastery over his corporeal desires.

He hadn't had the strength. Waiting until his wedding night, hanging on to control while he tried to understand her hesitation, had taken all his willpower. When he had been pushed right up to the edge and given the choice to protect himself or have her, he had chosen to have her.

Which told him everything he needed to know about how dangerous she was to him. Devastatingly dangerous.

Once hadn't been enough, either. Maybe if she

had expressed some reluctance or said she was tender, he might have restrained himself, but she had been as eager as him to bind their flesh irrevocably.

It wasn't until he woke in the dawn hours, aching to take her a fourth time, that sanity had intruded on the euphoria of honeymoon madness. She was slender, delectable, infinitely erotic but new to lovemaking. He *had* to find a shred of control, if only to continue calling himself human.

He left for his own apartment where he did everything he could to put himself back inside the armor he had worn until Galila had smashed him apart. He watched the sun come up, letting the brightness burn from his retina the image of her nubile curves. He listened to the morning numbers from overseas, drowning out the memory of her pleasured moans and cries. He showered the scent of her from his skin, then hated himself for all of it and wished himself back in her bed, feeling her warm, smooth skin stretching awake beside him.

He ordered their usual breakfast and had it served in the common dining room between their apartments, as it always was. He should have been sated and mellow. Instead, he was short on sleep and impatient with the staff as they hovered, each with their schedules and correspondence, their headlines and coffee urns.

Was the queen expected? Should they allow her to sleep? The questions were unending and struck him as unbearably intrusive. He gritted his teeth against ordering all of them out.

Despite his conflict, he lingered over his breakfast, full of self-loathing at the weakness he was displaying. His schedule had been emptied for the day after their reception as a courtesy. There was endless work in his office to be attended to and he shouldn't dally here like some besotted suitor, hoping to catch a glimpse of the object of his affection.

He was a man. One who ought to be in complete command of himself and the world around him. As he became aware of stirring behind the door to her room, he rose to leave.

* * *

Galila had barely been able to look at her own wan face in the mirror, feeling quite a chump for falling for Karim's promise. At least she had slept well past the time when he normally left for the far side of the palace. She would have the breakfast room to herself.

When she entered the small dining parlor, however, he was standing by the table, reviewing something on the tablet his aid was showing him. He flicked her a glance, one that lasted barely a second, but she saw the consternation in it. Read the lack of welcome in his stiff posture.

Waking alone had been a slap. Walking in here to see he had resumed his cloak of indifference was a kick in the stomach. Having all that play out before the usual assortment of hovering staff added insult to injury. Was it really necessary that she parade her deflowered self before a dozen people?

A case of acute vulnerability struck. Physically, she was fine. She'd had a bath and was only feeling as though she'd pushed herself with stretching poses, not particularly tender from their love-making. But memory of their intimacy thinned her skin. She couldn't bear to look at him, she was so dreading the coolness in his eyes.

"Good morning." She gathered her shredded composure and found a distant smile. "I thought you would be across the palace by now."

Silence.

She had the sense he was waiting for her to look at him, but she pretended to take enormous care with selecting cut fruit to add to her yogurt. She brushed away the serving hand that would have poured date syrup over her flatbread.

When she reached for the coffee urn, one of the staff hurried to fill her cup, but Karim said sharply, "I'll do it. Leave us."

His tone was so hard, Galila started, then remained on her guard, gaze on her untasted breakfast.

The room cleared in a quick shuffle of feet and a closed door.

She sat with her hands in her lap, discovering she was afraid to move. Not because she feared him, but because she had silently wished they were alone and now discovered the downside of that. No one to hide behind. She didn't want to move and draw his attention.

"You're angry with me," he said.

She was angry with herself.

"Why would you think that?" she murmured, picking up her spoon.

"You're not looking at me."

She should have looked at him then, to prove she wasn't avoiding it, but her eyes were hot. She feared he would read the anguish in them. She had poured out her heart to him last night. She had shared her body in a way she had never done with any other man and now...

"Even if I were..." *It wouldn't matter*, she wanted to say, but couldn't face that harsh reality so head-on. It would hurt too much. "Just go, Karim."

"I would have made love to you all night, Galila," he said through his teeth. "Until we were both too weak to move. As it was, I was far too rough with you. How do you feel?"

He hadn't sat down again and she only had the nerve to bring her gaze as far as the embroidery that edged his robe.

"Fine."

He sighed in a way that made her flinch, he sounded so impatient. Then he threw himself into the chair and his eyes were right there, leveled into hers like a strike of sunlight off water, penetrating so deep it hurt. Her eyes began to water and she blinked fast.

Through her wet lashes, she still saw the accusation behind his eyes. The way he searched her face as though trying to find a reason to hate her.

"I know a prevarication when I hear one," she said, her voice a scrape against the back of her throat. "You left because you'd had enough of me. Just go, Karim. It will be easier to stand being ignored if you're not doing it in person."

His hand closed into a fist. With a muttered curse, he unfurled it, then reached to take her wrist, the one that held her spoon. He tugged her to her feet and around the table where he pulled her into his lap.

She landed there stiffly, one elbow digging with resistance into his ribs, face forward as she gritted her teeth.

"What is this?" she demanded. "Some new form of torture where you assume that if I succumbed to you once, I'm yours whenever you want me?"

She very much feared she was. Her bones were already threatening to soften, her whole body wanting to relax into supple welcome, longing to melt into him, skin tingling for the sensation of his hands stroking over her.

"Definitely torture," he said, rubbing his beard into her neck so she shivered and squirmed in reaction.

His arms stayed locked around her, keeping her on his lap.

She put a little more pressure behind the sharpness of her elbow. "I'm actually hungry," she said pointedly.

"Eat, then," he invited, opening his arms and relaxing beneath her, but the way his hands settled on her hip and thigh told her he would restrain her if she tried to rise. "I will hold my wife and consider my inner failings."

"Sounds like I'll have time for dessert and a second cup of coffee." She didn't relax, still defensive even though his hands were settling, smoothing and massaging in a way that was kind of comforting, as though he wanted to offer and take pleasure in equal measures.

"Karim—"

"This is new territory for me, Galila. Don't expect my ease with this to happen overnight."

She let out a choke of humorless laughter. "Even though it was the deal you agreed to for that particular type of night? Are you just angling for more sex right now?"

His hands stalled. "Sex can wait until tonight."

Disappointment panged inside her even as he sighed toward the ceiling.

"I can stand depriving myself. Hurting you so badly you won't even look at me? That I cannot bear." His hands moved again, reassuring now then clenching possessively on her curves. "This level of passion isn't normal, you know. If you had had other lovers, you would know that and be as wary of it as I am." He dipped his head forward so his mouth was against her shoulder, whiskers tickling her skin.

She considered that as she spooned yogurt into her mouth. He wasn't offering her the open heart she wanted, but he was talking, at least. He had dismissed their audience. It was a small step, she supposed. One that allowed her to relax a little on his lap and enjoy the way he cradled her.

"You resent desiring me? That only makes me begrudge feeling attracted to you. That's not healthy, is it? Are we supposed to apologize for the pleasure we give each other?" She set petulant elbows on the table while she scraped at her yogurt bowl, deliberately jamming her buttocks deeper into his lap at the same time.

His hands gripped her hips and he drew a harsh breath.

She sent a knowing smirk into her bowl.

"Do you understand what you're inviting?" he asked mildly, opening his thighs a little so the shape of his aroused flesh dug firmly against her cheek.

"I believe you demonstrated that in great detail last night. Why do you think I'm so hungry? You'll have to let me finish my breakfast, though, before we satisfy other appetites. Otherwise, I'm liable to faint on you. Tell me something about yourself while you wait. What was your childhood like?"

"I didn't have one."

She started to rise, wanting to shift back to her own chair so she could look at him and gauge his expression as he spoke, but his hands hardened, keeping her on his lap. Keeping her with her back to him, she suspected.

"I didn't mean that to be an insensitive question," she said gently. "I thought, well, I supposed you might have played with cousins when you were young? Perhaps traveled when you were finishing your education?"

"My university was the throne of Zyria. When I wasn't with my tutors, I sat with my uncle, learning how to run my country. What did you do as a child?"

"Compared to that, it seems beyond childish. One of my favorite pastimes was learning pop songs. I have a decent voice and performed them for my mother's friends. I'm good with languages, too, which was another parlor trick she liked me to show off. I rode horses with my brothers and we camped in the desert with family sometimes. My childhood was fairly ideal. My teen years were more challenging."

"Why is that?"

She bit into the flatbread. It tasted like cardboard. For a moment, she thought about changing the subject, but maybe if he understood why she found his distance so hurtful...

"That's when she began to criticize me. I became obsessive about earning back her approval. I spent a ridiculous amount of time learning about fashion and makeup, trying to look more like her, thinking it would please her. I asked her to make every decision from my shade of lipstick to the shoes I wore. I kept thinking she couldn't disapprove of the way I looked if she made all my choices, but then she would say I was badgering her. Too needy. Everyone said it, my brothers especially. I felt like everyone hated me. It was awful."

Her scalp tickled as he idly played with her hair. "Did she send you away to Europe?"

"I begged my father to let me finish my schooling there. I couldn't take her moods. Even then, I was so careful to only be in the tabloids for good reasons. Helping a children's hospital or whatever. Anytime I received good press, though, she would say I was upstaging her. Begging for attention. There was no pleasing her."

She tried to twist and look at him, but he didn't let her. He continued playing with her hair, lightly tugging, dipping his nose to inhale, breathing out against the side of her neck.

"How are we talking about me?" she asked. "Tell me what you like about ruling Zyria."

"I like providing stability. No ruler can make an entire populace happy all the time. The best I can do is avoid war and ensure my people are not suffering in poverty. If they can eat and send their children to school, get the care they need and a new refrigerator when the old one breaks, then I am winning the game."

"That's true. You can't *make* someone happy. Do you ever wish you had brothers or sisters?"

He didn't answer. When she tried to turn her head to look at him, his hand tightened in her hair, preventing her. She gave a little shrug of warning, but he wasn't hurting her. He didn't let go, though. After a long minute, he answered.

"There are times I have thought my life would have been easier if I'd had an older brother and the responsibility I carry had gone to him," he spoke with a hint of dry humor, but his tone was also very grave. "Perhaps a lot of things would have been different. I don't know. But I can't make a sibling happen, so there's no point wishing for it."

She waited, but he didn't say anything else.

She pushed aside her emptied plate and sipped her coffee. When she set it down, he shifted her sideways so her legs were across his and they were finally looking at each other.

His face was impassive, difficult to read, but she understood him a little better. He carried a country on his shoulders and had for a long time. If he was lonely, he had made it his friend. That was why he was having such trouble turning to her.

Smoothing her hand over the silky hairs on his jaw, she said very sincerely, "Thank you for telling me that." She pecked his lips with hers.

The light kiss turned his dark eyes molten. "Are you sufficiently rejuvenated?"

"I could be talked into returning to the bedroom."

"Here will do."

Karim had to be extremely careful with his inquiries, but he had learned more about Adir. In the three weeks since Zufar's wedding, Adir had married Amira, the bride who had been promised to Galila's brother. Rumor had it they were expecting.

An odd pang had hit him with the news. For years, Karim had been ambivalent about procreating. More than one of his cousins had the temperament to rule. Was it latent sibling rivalry that prompted a sudden desire to make an heir?

"What's wrong?" Galila's soft voice nudged him back to awareness of the view off her balcony as her scent arrived to cloud around him.

He glanced back into her apartment and discovered her maids had finally left them alone.

In another lifetime, which was mere days ago, he would have brushed off her inquiry with a brisk and conscienceless "Nothing." He wasn't required to explain his introspective moods to anyone.

But Galila's slender arms came around his waist as she inserted herself under his arm. Her pointy chin rested on his chest and she gazed up at him. The pretty bat of her lashes was an invitation to cast off his pensiveness and confide in her.

"There are things I would discuss with you if I could, but I can't," he said, surprised to discover it was true. He wanted to confide in her. It was yet another disturbing shift in his priorities. "It's confidential." He stroked the side of his thumb against her soft cheek to cushion his refusal.

"Hmm," she said glumly. "Bad?"

"Not violent, if that's what you mean."

"Trade embargoes or something," she guessed.

Did not acknowledging his potential successor to Zyria's throne count as an embargo? "Something like that."

"You can trust me, you know. I know I behaved indiscreetly the night we met, but I'm not usually so reckless. That was a special case. With a special man," she added, lips tilting into the smile that he fell for like a house of cards.

She hadn't had a drop of alcohol since the night they met, he had noted.

She shifted so they were front to front and rested her ear on his chest, sighing with contentment. His hands went to her back of their own accord, exploring her warm shape through the silk robe she wore over her nightgown.

This was becoming the norm for him—holding her. He wasn't a dependent man, but she was so tactile and affectionate, seeming to thrive on his touch, he couldn't resist petting and cuddling her.

"I don't regret telling you about him that night. Adir, I mean," she murmured.

He stalled in stroking across her narrow shoulders.

"I'm glad you're willing to listen. That *I* can trust *you*," she went on. "I'm still so shocked by Mother's affair and Adir. I keep wondering about Amira. How she even knew Adir well enough she would run away with him."

He almost told her the woman was married and expecting, but she would wonder how he came to know it.

"Did you know her well?" he asked instead, resuming his massage across her back.

"Her father is one of my father's oldest friends. She was promised to Zufar since she was born. I was looking forward to having her as a sister-in-law. And Zufar—you saw him on a really bad day. He can be gruff, but he would have done his best to be a good husband. I've asked him what he has learned of Adir, but he's so angry, he wants nothing to do with it. I don't know what to do. I want to be sure Amira is well and happy with her decision, but I can't very well make inquiries without spilling our family secrets, can I?" She leaned back to regard him. "See? I am capable of discretion."

"I'll see what I can learn," he promised, pleased when she grew visibly moved.

"You will? Thank you!"

He was growing so soft. He very much feared he was becoming infatuated with his wife, constantly wanting to put that light in her expression and feel her throw her arms around him like he was her savior.

He picked her up and took her to the bed, distantly wondering what she would say when he told her he had learned her friend was pregnant.

I don't desire your children.

He didn't know why that continued to sting when they made love so passionately every night. It was early days in their marriage and he ought to be pleased they were making love frequently without morning sickness or other health concerns curtailing their enjoyment of each other.

Still, as they stripped and began losing themselves in each other, he was aware of a deeper hunger that went beyond the drive for sexual satisfaction. Beyond his need to feel her surrender to him and take such joy at his touch. He wanted all of her. Every ringing cry, every dark thought, every tear and smile and whispered secret.

He suspected he wanted her heart.

Do I look pretty, Mama?

Galila was in the gown she intended to wear to stand next to her mother at the children's hospital gala. This used to be one of their favorite events, but for months now, her mother had been growing more and more critical. Galila didn't understand why.

She had tried very, very hard this time to be utterly flawless. Her gown was fitted perfectly to her growing bust and scrupulously trim waistline. Her hair fell in big barrel curls around her shoulders. Her makeup was light, since her mother still thought she was too young—at sixteen!—to wear it. Nail polish had been allowed for years, though. She had matched hers to the vibrant pink of her gown and wore heels, something the queen had also been arguing were too old for her.

She thought she looked as beautiful as she possibly could and smiled with hope, trying to prompt an answering one from her mother's stiff expression.

Her mother winced and gave her a pitying look. *I expect you to have better instincts, Galila. The green would be better and a nude shade on your lips.*

Rejection put a searing ache in the back of Galila's throat. She turned away to hide how crushed she was, waiting until her mother went back into her own closet before she reached for a tissue on the shelf and dabbed it beneath her eyes, trying to keep her makeup from running.

Why was her mother being so cruel lately? She stared blindly at the bookshelf, trying to make sense of her mother's change in attitude. She used to be all purrs and strokes, now she was claws and hisses. Just like…

The object before her blurred eyes came into focus. It was a bookend. Two slabs of ebony with a bright gold figure upon it. A lioness. She stood on her hind legs, one paw braced against the upright wall as she peered over the top, as if looking for her mate—

Galila sat up with a terrified gasp beside him, jolting Karim awake.

"What is it?" He reached out a hand in the dark, finding her naked back coated in sweat. The bumps of her spine stood up as she curled her back, hugging her knees protectively. Her heartbeat slammed into his palm from behind her ribs, drawing him fully out of slumber.

"Nightmare?" he guessed. "Come here. You're safe."

She only hugged herself into a tighter ball, tucking her face into her knees, back rising and falling as she dragged long breaths into her lungs, as though she was being pursued.

He came up on an elbow, and rubbed her back, trying to ensure she was as awake as he was. "Are you in pain?"

"Just a bad dream." She didn't let him draw her under the covers, though. She pressed a clammy hand to his chest and pushed her feet toward the edge of the mattress. All of her shook violently, her reaction so visceral, his own body responded with a small release of adrenaline. He caught at her arm, ready to protect her against frightening shadows and monsters under the bed.

"What was it about?"

"I need a minute. Let me—" She left the bed and found her silk robe, pulling it on before she disappeared into the bathroom.

He was sleeping inordinately well these days, thanks to their regular and passionate lovemaking. The sated, sluggish beast in him wanted to lie back and drift into unconsciousness again, but he heard water running.

Concerned, he rose and followed her into the bathroom where the light blinded him. She had turned on the tap and buried her face in a towel to muffle her sobs. The cries were so violent, they racked her shoulders.

His scalp tightened. This reaction was off the scale. "Galila."

She hadn't heard him come in and gasped, lifting a face that was so white, his heart swerved in his chest.

"You look like a ghost," he said. Or she'd seen one. He tried to take her in his arms, but she wouldn't allow it.

"I'm sorry. I can't—" Her words ended in a choke. She set aside the towel and splashed the water on her face, then dried it only to hide behind the dark blue cloth again.

Her desire for distance surprised him. Stung, even. He was used to her turning to him for the least thing. He liked it.

"What was it about?" he insisted. "Tell me."

She couldn't. She was barely making sense of it herself. She wasn't even sure if it was a genuine memory. Dreams were pure imagination, weren't they?

Clenching her eyes shut, she tried to recall her mother's boudoir. Her bookshelves. Was it possible the lioness she had pictured so clearly had been conjured by the curiosity that was plaguing her? She wanted to know who her mother's lover had been, so she was inventing scenarios in her sleep.

Or was it real? The palace of her childhood was full of objets d'art. Masterpieces in oil, ivory, ceramic and yes, some were sculptures cast in gold. Could she mentally picture all of them? Of course not, especially the ones that had been in her parents' private rooms. She hadn't entered those much at all.

But she *had* gone to her mother that one afternoon, ahead of the children's hospital ball. That was a real memory. She distinctly remembered it because the ball had fallen right after her birthday. The pink gown had been a present to herself, one she had been certain her mother would approve of.

None of that was the reason she could hardly catch her breath, however.

What if it is true? What if her mother had owned the other side of Karim's father's lion bookend? Did that prove Karim's father had been her lover? Or was it a bizarre coincidence?

"Galila."

Karim's tone demanded she obey him.

She opened her eyes and searched his gaze, but couldn't bring herself to ask if it was possible. How would he know? He'd been a child. And the suspicion was so awful, such a betrayal to his mother, she didn't want to speculate about it herself, let alone put it on him to wonder.

What would such an accusation do to this tentative connection they had formed? She couldn't bear to lose what was growing between them. He had married her to be a link between their two countries, not the catalyst for a rift that couldn't be mended.

With lashes wet with helplessness, she said very truthfully, "I don't want to think of it." She held out her hand. "Make love to me," she whispered. "Make me forget."

He was too sharp not to recognize she was putting him off, but he let her plaster herself across his front and draw his head down to kiss him.

Within seconds, he took command of their lovemaking, taking her back to bed where they were both urgent in a way that was new and agonizing, as if he felt the pull of conflict within her. Impending doom. He dragged his mouth down her body, pleasured her to screaming pitch and kept her on the edge of ecstasy, then rolled her onto her knees. She gripped the headboard in desperate hands as he thrust into her from behind, but even after she shuddered in release, he wasn't done. He aroused her all over again, his own body taut and hotter than a branding iron when he finally settled over her and drew her thighs to his waist.

Now he was everything, her entire world, filling her, possessing her, driving her to new heights that they reached together, so intense she sobbed in glory.

Spent, she fell asleep in his arms, clinging to his damp body as if he could save her from her own subconscious.

But the lioness stalked her into the morning light.

When she woke, she knew what she had to do.

"Are you sure you're all right?" Karim asked twice over breakfast. It was usually a private meal now. He let their aids in when they were nursing their second cup of coffee, rarely before. "You'll feel better if you talk it out."

"It's silly," she prevaricated, but couldn't find the dismissive smile she needed. "Just a silly dream."

He knew she was lying to him. She could tell by the grim frown overshadowing his stern gaze. It chilled her heart to disappoint him and even worse, deserve his consternation.

"I don't want to relive it," she said, miserable at not being able to share.

His mouth twitched with dismay, but he let the subject drop. A few minutes later, he rose to start his day.

When she was certain he was on the far side of the palace, she texted Niesha, Zufar's wife and the new Queen of Khalia. With so much going on, she had barely absorbed her brother's email yesterday concerning his new wife and the startling possibility she could be the lost Princess of Rumadah.

It wouldn't have surprised her in the least if Niesha hadn't returned her message, preferring to take time to absorb her own life changes, but she video-called Galila a short time later. Galila dismissed the maid in her room and answered, forcing herself to strike a casual pose on the end of a sofa, as if she wasn't wound so tightly with nerves she was ready to snap. It took everything in her to get through a few gentle inquiries after Niesha's situation and well-being.

"Thank you so much for calling me back," Galila said when she felt she could steer the conversation to her own interests. "I don't know what made me think of a particular keepsake of my mother's, but I wondered if it was on the shelf in your room? Would you be able to show me? It's an ebony bookend with a lioness cast in gold."

"I'm so sorry," Niesha said. "All her rooms have

been completely redecorated, but your mother's things were boxed up and put into storage. Nothing was discarded. It's all safe."

"No apology is necessary. Of course, you made it your own." Galila spared a brief thought for how odd it must be for Niesha to be living as a queen, rather than a maid. They were equals now and Galila had to remember that, but she was fixated on learning the truth. "Do you recall seeing a bookend with a lioness, though?"

"I don't recall it, no. Let me check with Zufar. I'm sure he'll agree you should be the one to have her things. I'll have them shipped to you."

It wasn't exactly the answer she wanted. Galila had hoped to solve the mystery in seconds. Instead, she had to act like it was a trifling thing, not an obsessive worry.

"Whenever you have time," she said with a flick of her hand. "I don't want to disturb you when you have so much going on."

The more Galila thought about it, however, the more she was convinced that Karim's father, King Jamil, had been her mother's lover. The timing fit with Adir's age and her own father's diplomatic tour. A brief glance at Zyria's history online confirmed that Karim's father had died very shortly after her father had returned to Zyria.

Had his death been a catalyst for her mother telling her father about her pregnancy? Had Jamil's accident even been an accident?

She couldn't help dwelling on every possibility as she waited for the boxes to arrive.

What if Karim's father had been her mother's lover? That would mean Adir was Karim's half brother, too. How would he react to *that* news?

Not that she could burden him with any of this. Definitely not until she had more evidence than a spooky dream.

But if it did turn out to be true, was it wise to tell him? He would have to keep it from his mother, who still held Jamil so close to her heart. What of the political ramifications? Zufar was already dealing with an embittered man who blamed him for the loss of his birthright. She couldn't subject Karim to the same.

A sensible woman would leave the mystery unsolved, but she couldn't let it go. At the same time, keeping all of this inside her was like trying to ignore an abscess. It throbbed and ached in the back of her throat, flaring up and subsiding as she pretended to Karim that she was fine, all the while waiting on tenterhooks for news that the shipment of boxes had arrived.

A week later, rather than bother Niesha again, she had her assistant speak to the palace in Khalia. The boxes had finally left and should arrive in a day or two.

Somehow, knowing they were on their way was far worse than if they hadn't left.

"Should I cancel our dinner engagement tonight?" Karim asked over breakfast.

"Pardon?" Galila's gaze came back from staring at nothing and focused on him. She seemed to become aware that her coffee was halfway to her mouth and set it down without tasting it. "Why would you do that?" she asked.

Because she had been positively vacant the last

few days. He wanted to know why. This was usually her favorite time of day, when she had him all to herself. She usually flirted and chattered, reminded him to call his mother and asked if he had any preferences for upcoming menu choices. She might sidle up to his chair and kiss him if she was feeling particularly sensual.

She'd become downright remote of late, though. He hated it.

"You're not yourself. Is there something we should discuss?"

"What? No! I'm completely fine." A blatant lie. "Just…distracted. Should I let the staff in?" She rose to do it.

"Does it have to do with Adir? Because I have news."

"You do?" She swung back, interest sharp.

"He married Amira. She's expecting. Sooner than one would anticipate, given she was supposed to marry your brother a month ago," he added drily. "My reports are that they're quite happy."

"Oh. I thought she must have had some sort of

relationship with him, to be willing to go with him like that. It's good to know she's well." She stood with her hands linked before her, still taking it in, chewing her lip and pleating her brow. "That's all you learned?"

For some reason, the way her gaze searched his caused the hair on the back of his neck to stand up.

"Yes." The word *why?* stayed locked in his throat.

With a thoughtful nod, she let in their staff, curtailing further discussion.

Galila wanted the lion on hand to compare to the lioness when—*if*—it arrived. Would Karim miss it if she removed it from his study? At the very least, she needed a fresh look at it. She wanted to search for a signature or an identifying engraving or seal—anything that might prove it was one of a pair.

She would take a few photos on her phone, she decided, as she crossed to the far side of the palace.

Karim had left their breakfast room about an hour ago for his day of royal duties. Would he cancel their dinner? She wasn't sure how she felt about that. Her mind was a whirlwind these days, one where she could barely take in what Karim had said about Adir and Amira when she was so focused on discovering who Adir's father was. Obviously her distraction was beginning to show, but she couldn't tell Karim what was bothering her until she could provide a definitive answer.

Much like the first time when she had arrived without warning, she was invited to wait in his study. She again insisted he should not be interrupted. She wanted to be alone for this.

The bookend was exactly where she had seen it the first time. It was surprisingly heavy. She turned it this way and that on the shelf, taking photos, then tilted it to look at the bottom.

There was a date that fell a few weeks into Galila's father's trip away. The artist was someone she didn't know, but she would look up the name later. Where was he located? Zyria? Khalia? Somewhere in between where lovers might meet?

Most tellingly, the piece was called *Where Is She?*

Her heart began to thump as she instinctively guessed the other would be called *Where Is He?*

"They just told me you were waiting."

Karim's voice startled her so badly she dropped the bookend, narrowly missing her foot and crying out with alarm as she leaped back from it.

"Did it hit you?" Karim grasped at her arm to steady her, then crouched, trying to examine her foot.

Galila stumbled back, certain her guilty conscience gleamed bright as full moon on a clear night. "I'm fine," she stammered. "Did I break it? I'm so sorry. I didn't hear you come in."

"Worry about your foot." He picked up the bookend and rose, turning it over and weighing it in his hand. "I don't think a nuclear bomb could hurt this thing, but you would be in a cast if it had landed on your toes. What was so engrossing about it?"

"I don't know," she babbled, finding it increasingly impossible to lie to him, especially when she had been working so hard to coax him to open up to her. "It's just a very well-crafted piece, don't you think?"

He narrowed his eyes and studied it more closely, reading the bottom before slowly setting it on the shelf and nudging it up against the books.

"It belonged to your father, I imagine? I would feel horrible if I had dented it."

"It's fine." He folded his arms and frowned at her. "What did you need?"

"I—" She couldn't say *Nothing*. Not when she had said she needed to speak to him and would wait here for a private audience. Last night, when she had decided to come here to examine the bookend, she had conjured a question about Adir and Amira, but he had answered that this morning. They had private conversations every day over breakfast. She had no good excuse for being here.

Fighting to keep her gaze from drifting back to the lion, she racked her brain.

"Is it whatever you've been hiding from me?"

Her heart took a hard bounce, causing her voice to stutter. "W-what?"

She knew damned well her gaze was rife with culpability as it rose to his. She watched his own narrow like a predatory bird swooping into a nose dive.

"You think I can't tell? We're so attuned, I sense the slightest shift in the cadence of your breath and the change of scent on your skin. You're worried about something. You avoid my eyes—" He muttered an imprecation. "You're doing it now. *Look at me.*"

She couldn't. Guilt weighed her lashes along with her shoulders and even her head on her neck. She couldn't tell him, though. Not until she knew for sure.

This morning, when he had mentioned Adir, she had wondered if he had learned Adir was his half brother. Now, through her panic, she recalled something else that had penetrated the edges of her mind during that conversation. A suspicion that had been overshadowed by her turmoil over a pair of bookends.

It was something she wasn't quite ready to acknowledge because she could be just as wrong about that as she might be about his father. But she would rather speculate on that than the other.

"I think I'm pregnant."

CHAPTER EIGHT

KARIM HEARD THE words but they didn't make sense. They weren't bad, just astonishing. "How?"

She rolled her eyes. "Do not tell me to have 'the talk' with you. Not the way we've been carrying on."

He couldn't help smirking at that, but then frowned in confusion. "I said you could use birth control. You said you wanted to."

"Yes, well." She wrinkled her nose and gave her hair a self-conscious flip. "I was annoyed with you the day I came in here to discuss that. The doctor was very patronizing, making it sound like I *had* to take something. As if it was your decision that I shouldn't conceive. You'll recall that we weren't even having sex at the time..." She looked at her manicure, embarrassed by her pique that day, but also blushing at how uninhibited she'd been with him.

"I remember." His voice held a warm, delicious undertone, one that made her toes curl. "So you didn't go on anything?"

"I had a small tantrum about it at the doctor's, then came here. I kept thinking I should go back and get it sorted, but I don't care for him, so I never did."

"He's been my doctor all my life. He's very thorough."

"And I'm sure you would enjoy discussing your personal life with my female doctor back in Khalia, who is also very thorough," she said pertly.

"Point taken. See if she wants to relocate."

"I've had preliminary discussions about the women's health center and met some excellent female doctors here in Nabata. I only have to ask my assistant to book me an appointment, but—you're going to think me the biggest idiot alive, Karim. You're going to say I'm the one who needed 'the talk.'"

"Why?" He frowned.

"I honestly didn't think it would happen so fast," she admitted with a groan. "I've been ignoring the signs because I feel quite stupid for thinking I could have sex and get around to starting birth control when I felt like making a visit to a new doctor a priority. I'm a grown woman. *I know better.*"

He laughed. It was a brief chuckle that was more of a pair of staccato exhales, but it made her insides blossom in sweetly smug triumph for squeezing that carefree noise out of him.

His amusement lingered in his expression as he shook his head in wry disbelief at her. In fact, he was so handsome in that moment, she tipped a little further into love with him.

A little further? Oh, dear. Yes. She was quite in love with him, she realized with a stutter of her heart. She looked to the floor, letting her hair fall forward to curtain her face and hide that she was coming to terms with a *lot* lately. How had she been so foolish as to do that though? The very thing she feared most—yearning for someone she loved to love her back—was now the definition of her marriage.

With that burning ache for a return of her affections pressing outward in the base of her throat, she asked, "Are you angry?"

"Of course not! I'm astounded, but thrilled. You told me you didn't desire my children."

"I was angry." She wrinkled her nose in apology. "It turns out, I do want your baby, Karim. Very much." So much, the magnitude of it pushed bright tears into her eyes.

His expression of utter bemusement turned tender as he cupped her face. His gaze was quite solemn.

"I've been thinking lately that we ought to be trying to conceive, waiting for the right time to bring it up. I'm very happy with this news, Galila. I only wish you had felt you could trust me with it sooner. Is this why you've been so distracted? You thought I wouldn't approve?"

She shrugged, feeling evasive as she buried her face in his shoulder, but enormous feelings were overtaking her. Love, a kind she had never before experienced, had a breadth and depth that terrified even as it exhilarated her. Anticipation of their growing family swelled excitedly in her while profound despair countered her buoyancy. He had said he would never love her. Overshadowing all of that was the secret of his father's possible affair with her mother, the weight of it heavy enough to crush her flat.

He closed his arms around her, though, and kissed her with such incredible sweetness, her world righted itself for a few precious seconds.

"I'm glad you're pleased," she said against his mouth.

"That's two good memories you've given me in this room to replace my bad one."

She was so startled by that statement she drew back and studied him.

He clearly regretted his remark at once. She watched his expression close up. His jaw hardened and his lips sealed themselves into a tight line.

Ah, this man of hers. He was capable of opening up, but only in very brief and narrow peeks.

She traced the hollow of his rigid spine through his shirt, saying quietly, "I wondered."

He grimaced and his gaze struck the curtains that hid the balcony beyond.

"Do you have many memories of him? Six is so young."

"Too young for a memory like that," he said flatly, almost as if he'd seen his father's body, but surely not. Who would allow such a thing?

She started to ask, but he kissed each of her eyes closed. "Shall we make another pleasant memory in here?" His mouth sought hers.

She let him erase the troubling thoughts lingering in her psyche, but it was temporary. She hadn't been completely honest with him and couldn't be.

Not until she had found the lion's mate.

Galila belatedly realized how tasteless it was to have her mother's things shipped to her in Zyria. She wound up requesting they be left in a storage room in the lower palace, rather than in the royal chambers.

Then she had to wait until she had a free afternoon, which didn't happen until she had had her doctor's appointment and her pregnancy confirmed.

That had prompted a flurry of additional appointments with key staff who would keep the news confidential but begin preparations for the upcoming heir. She and Karim even squeezed in a day trip to inform his mother, who was beside herself at the news.

Finally, five days later, Galila was able to go with her assistant down to the roomful of boxes and begin sifting through them. They were labeled but very generally—Books, Art and Heirlooms—all words that could indicate the box held the bookend she sought.

Her assistant was beginning to nag her about being on her feet too long when she squeezed something hard and vaguely animal-shaped through a careful wrapping of linen. She asked her helpers to leave her alone for a few moments.

Stomach tight and curdling, she lifted out the

heavy piece. Her hands shook as she unwound the linen.

It was the lioness, exactly as she had dreamed it.

Not risking her foot this time, she kept it on the table and tilted it enough to see the same artist's signature, the same date and the inscription *Where Is He?*

She drew a shaken breath. What should she do now?

Galila was still not herself. Was it the baby? Karim wondered.

She had had the pregnancy confirmed and the obvious signs were there, now that he made a point to notice them. She hadn't had a cycle and her breasts were tender. A brief glance online told him moodiness and forgetfulness weren't uncommon.

If he didn't know better, however, he would think she was drunk, she was so absentminded, leaving the making of conversation with their guests to him. He could tell the older couple was surprised by her wan smiles and quiet introspection. They had met her before and knew she was typically animated and engaging.

Finally, the wife of the minister said something about Galila suffering the pressure of producing an heir. Galila snapped out of her daze to blush and Karim was certain they immediately put her distraction down to pregnancy. They left with smug smiles, convinced they held a state secret.

"Our news will be rumored on every station tomorrow," he said as he followed her into her rooms.

She gave him a startled look. "What news?"

He stared at her. "What is going on with you?"

Her entire being seemed to deflate. "I have to talk to you about something and I don't know how."

The anguish in her expression made his heart lurch. "Is it the baby?"

How could he be instantly devastated when he'd barely begun to absorb this new reality?

"No. I'm perfectly fine. Not even iron deficient or suffering much morning sickness. The baby and I are completely healthy. No, this is something else entirely." She touched her forehead. "Come. I have to show you something."

They dismissed the staff and she took him into her bedroom where she knelt to open a lower drawer. She lifted out a wrapped object that was obviously heavy.

He bent to take it from her and saw the anxiety that leaped into her expression as he picked it up, as if she wanted to snatch it back.

"What is it?" Its density and bulk felt vaguely familiar.

She waved at the bed and he set it there to let her unwrap it. She did, slowly. With dread, even. He heard her swallow as she revealed glimpses of ebony and gold.

It was a bookend, one he recognized as similar to the one that had so engrossed her in his office. The two polished black slabs set at an angle were identical to his, but the lioness cast in gold on this one was in a different position, peering over the top of the wall, rather than around the side.

She had distracted him with pregnancy news,

but that had been subterfuge. *This* had been her reason for coming to his office last week. He didn't care to be lied to, but that wasn't what made his scalp prickle so hard it felt as though it was coming off.

"An early birthday present?" He wasn't a flippant man. The remark came out abraded by the gravel in his throat. The pit of his gut was turning sour. "Where did it come from?"

He already knew, even before she looked up at him with misery and regret pulling at her features. Her knuckles were white and sharp as teeth where she clutched the linen in her fist.

"It belonged to my mother."

He closed his eyes. Now came the fury.

"Who else have you told?"

Galila frowned in confusion. "What do you mean, who have I told? Karim, do you understand what I'm telling *you*?"

"Yes," he clipped out.

She had expected more disbelief and shock, not an immediate leap to damage control. She had agonized all day, since pulling this from the box, about whether to tell him. She had then braced herself for having to convince him, once he realized what she suspected. This was, after all, circumstantial evidence. Strong but not definitive. Of course, he would have doubts. She still wasn't ready to believe it.

How could he get there so fast without working through all the reasons that this proved nothing?

"Maybe you should sit down," she said. "Because I don't think you realize what this might mean."

"It matches the one that belonged to my father. *I know what it means*, Galila. I didn't think there was proof of their affair. That there was a way for it to be pieced together. What did you tell them in Khalia about this?" His voice was scythe-sharp, cutting off her reach for other explanations and leaving her weak excuses on the ground. He was so tall and intimidating in that moment, she stumbled back a step.

She kept going, backing away until her knees

found the chair where she threw her robe when she climbed into bed. She plopped into it.

"Am I to understand you *knew*?" She was like a fish gasping for air, jaw working, eyes goggling.

"Of course I knew! Why do you think I married you?"

She was glad she was sitting down. His words bowled her over. She felt each of the buttons in the upholstery digging into her back.

"That's why you came on to me at Zufar's wedding? Why you coerced him into agreeing to our marriage? To hide this secret?" She thought being a political pawn had been bad. She wasn't even *that* expedient! Their marriage was a gag order, nothing more.

"Do you understand the ramifications if this gets out?" he went on. "It could start a war!"

She had never seen him this aggressive, shoulders bunched, face so hard there was nothing of the tender lover she had slept beside. He was not a man at all. He was a warrior defending his kingdom.

"My parents' marriage was a peace treaty with

tribesmen who backed her father," he added in a clipped tone. "They support me, but grudgingly. If they found out my father cheated on her? That he had a child with another woman? Who knows what sort of retaliation they would take against me. Or Adir."

He paced away and his hand cut through the air.

"Who even knows what kind of man Adir is? He's already shown himself willing to take revenge against your brother for your mother's actions. What would he do to me and Zyria? Then there is your brother Zufar."

He spun to confront her.

"Zyria and Khalia have been in a cold war for years. Your mother's doing, I am sure, since my uncle's overtures after my father's death were always shut down. *I* knew why the relationship between our countries went stale." He tapped the center of his chest. "I never tried to reach out when I took the throne, knowing there was no point. But after your mother passed, I was suddenly invited to your brother's wedding. We are finally in a position to mend fences between our countries and you want to tell him *this*?"

"No!" she cried. "I haven't told Zufar or anyone. I've been agonizing about telling *you*." She had been trying to protect him, didn't he see that?

"How you even—" He ran his hand down his face and glared at the bookend.

"How did *you* know?" she asked.

"My father told me," he spat with great bitterness. "The night he died. Your mother cut off their affair and he got himself blind drunk. If only he had blacked out, but no. He sat there and told me in great detail how deeply he was suffering a broken heart. Said he loved my mother, but not the way he loved Namani. His feelings for her were beyond what he thought possible."

His tortured memory of that night threw harsh shadows into his face.

"He'd thought she felt the same, but she broke it off. He couldn't go on without her. Refused to."

Galila tried to speak and realized her hand was over her mouth. She lowered it. "You were six years old What was he thinking, putting all of that on you?"

"He wasn't thinking. He was out of his mind with agony."

Karim's own agony was written in deep lines of anguished grief, painful memory and a lifetime of confusion and regret.

"It was years before I understood it properly, but he wanted me to know why he was leaving it all in my hands. He couldn't leave a note. My mother would have seen it."

"Are you saying—Karim," she breathed, gripping the arms of her chair and leaning forward. "His death was deliberate." *Please, no.*

He flashed one tortured flare of his gaze her direction, then showed her his grim profile. "My mother can never know. I've always let her believe he stumbled."

"You *saw* that?" The words tore a strip from the back of her heart to the back of her throat, leaving a streak of burning anguish on his behalf. "That's horrible! He never should have—"

Her entire composure was crumpling in empathy for him. She rose anyway, but he stiffened as she approached, telling her he didn't want her comfort. It was an excruciating rejection.

"Karim…" She held out a hand. "I had to tell you, but I would never, ever tell anyone any of this. Certainly not your mother."

He jerked his chin in a nod of acknowledgment, but when she came closer, he again stiffened and held up a hand this time, warding her off.

His harshly voiced declaration came back to her. *Why do you think I married you?* Surely, they had built something beyond that, though? She was carrying his child.

"I'm going to put that in my personal safe," he said. "I don't want anyone else to see it and come to the same conclusions you have."

"Of course." She moved to take up the linen, but he took it from her and wrapped it himself, disappearing to his own side.

She stood there waiting for his return. And waited and waited.

He didn't come back.

* * *

Galila entered the breakfast room to find a handful of aides doing exactly what her husband wanted them to do—they were creating a buffer between him and his wife.

She had spent a restless night missing his heat beside her in the bed, trying to take in the fact Karim had known all along that his father had had an affair with her mother. That he had lied to her about his reasons for marrying her and hadn't trusted her enough to tell her the truth. Not until she figured it out for herself.

Now she had, he was turning his back on her again. Why? Shouldn't this shared secret draw them closer?

As she sank into her chair, he rose, almost as if they were on different ends of a child's seesaw.

"I have a busy morning," he said, looking to the door rather than at her. "If you have questions about our schedule with the duke and duchess, we should cover that now, before we greet them at the airport."

Why do you think I married you?

They had grown close despite his initial motives, though. Hadn't they? He had seemed happy about her pregnancy. Until last night, they had made love unreservedly. That meant she was a source of pleasure for him, didn't it? Surely, he felt *something* toward her? He wasn't going to reject her out of hand, now that she had uncovered the truth about his father's infidelity. Was he?

He didn't give her time to ask any of her questions, rushing out to start his day. They were both tied up for the next few days as they hosted several dignitaries around an international competition for child athletes recovering from land mines and other war-related injuries.

Galila did what she had done for years. She ensured her appearance was scrupulously balanced between flawless elegance and warm benevolence. The cameras adored her. All of Zyria praised Karim for his choice in bride. They dubbed her the Queen of Compassion.

She was miserable, taking no pleasure in the adulation. Thankfully, the car windows were tinted and the madly waving crowd couldn't see that she wore such a long face.

Karim finished his call beside her, one he hadn't needed to make. It was yet another brick in the wall he was building against her.

Before he could cement another into place, she asked, "Are you so angry with me for figuring it out that you can't even speak to me about it?"

He paused in placing another call. "There's nothing left to say."

"Is there nothing left of our marriage, either? Because you're avoiding me. You're—" He was avoiding their bed.

He sighed. It was the sigh that cut through her like a blade. *Don't be needy*, it said.

"Why aren't you sleeping with me?" She swung her face toward him, refusing to guess at his reasons. "Is it because I'm pregnant? Because you don't trust me? Because you're angry? What did I do to make you turn your back on me, Karim?"

"Nothing," he said from behind clenched teeth. "I was simply reminded by our…discussion the other night that…" He polished the screen of his phone on his thigh. "This passion between us is dangerous," he stated more firmly.

She studied his craggy profile. He was staring straight ahead at the closed privacy window. There might as well be one between them, holding her apart from his thoughts and feelings. From his heart.

"Is that all it is?" She felt as though she inched onto thin ice. "Because I had begun to hope it was more than merely passion."

His jaw pulsed. "I told you not to expect that."

Don't be needy.

Swallowing, she looked to the palm trees that lined the boulevard as they approached the palace. The archway and fountain, the flower garden and flags, the columns and carpeted steps that formed the impressive entrance of the Zyrian palace.

He offered her a home as beautiful as the one she'd grown up in, and as equally empty of love.

"Why?" Her voice broke. "I don't understand why I should never expect to feel loved, Karim.

What is wrong with me that I must lower my expectations and stop believing I deserve that?"

"It's not you." The car stopped and he said, "I don't want to talk about this right now."

"You don't want to talk about it ever. Be honest about that much, please." She slid out of the car as the door was opened for her.

Karim threw himself from the far side and flashed her a look across the roof of the car, one that accused her of pushing him to the very limits of his control.

"You want me to be honest? Come, then." He snapped his fingers at her as he started down the walkway alongside the palace.

She knew eyes followed them, but they were left to walk alone through the garden and around the corner of the public wing to the side of the palace that faced the sea. Here the grounds were a narrow band of beach, a triangle of garden and a courtyard—

Oh. She realized where they were when he stopped in the middle of a ruthlessly straight path and looked upward.

"Karim," she breathed. The sun beat down on them so hot it dried the air in her lungs. Her shoulders stung through the silk of her dress and her scalp tingled as though burning along the part in her hair.

"He was so *in love*—" his inflection made the emotion sound like a case of leprosy "—he could not live without her. He preferred to plunge to his death, *in front of his son*, than face another day without her. Is that what you want me to feel for you, Galila? Unable to live without you?"

The reflection off the building was so hot it burned her face, even though the sun was behind her.

"They weren't able to be together." And she knew her mother. There was every chance she didn't love Jamil in the same way, not that she would dare say so. "Our situation is different. I—I'm falling in love with you."

His body jolted as though struck. "Do not," he said grittily. "We have the foundation for something that can work. If we hold ourselves at arm's length."

"No, we don't!" She grabbed his sleeve and shook his arm, as if she could shake some sense into him. "We almost did and now you're pushing me away again. Karim, are you really saying you will never love me? That you would rather break *my* heart by refusing to? By your logic, that means I should go drown myself right now." She thumbed toward the nearby waves washing the shore.

His gaze flashed from her to the water. He flinched, then his expression hardened. "I'm putting a stop to your feelings before they get any worse."

Worse? He really didn't understand love at all. Which was, perhaps, the real problem.

"You aren't just refusing to love me, you *can't*. Can you?" He didn't know how.

"Cannot and will not. I'm protecting both of us. All of Zyria."

He had told her this before, but some tiny thing inside her—smaller even than the child she carried—had hoped. Now she knew how foolish that hope had been. Now she believed him when he said he would never love her.

Her next breath was deep. It was the kind one took to absorb the sting of a deep cut or the reverberation from a cracked head. The kind that felt like a knife going into her throat and staying there.

"Very well, then."

CHAPTER NINE

KARIM ROSE AND prowled through the dark to the door to Galila's bedroom, paused, turned back and sat in the chair, elbows braced on his splayed thighs.

He was hard, so hungry for her he was sweating and panting with need, but he made himself resist the lure of her. The weakness that going to her would represent.

She might not welcome him anyway. He had ground her heart beneath his heel a few days ago and she'd been walking around like a ghost ever since. He loathed himself for doing it, but clung to the truth he had spoken. They had a child on the way. He had to keep a level head on his shoulders for the next two decades, at least.

Two decades of meting out their lovemaking in small measures to prove to himself he didn't need her like air and water. Twenty years of averting his gaze from her laughing expression so he wouldn't be tempted. Of listening to the falsely cheerful tone she used when she was hurting and trying not to let it show.

Of knowing he was breaking her heart.

She had said she was falling in love with him.

He closed his eyes, savoring those words before pushing them to the furthest reaches of his consciousness. Whatever she felt was so new, she would be able to recover from his rejection. He was sure of it.

He had to believe it.

Unable to sleep and quite sure he would go to her if he stayed, he dressed and went to his office across the palace. It wasn't even sunrise. He ate an early breakfast in his library, a room where she permeated the walls, layering over old memories like a clean coat of paint, then started his work day.

He was little better than a ghost himself, unable to say later what he had accomplished. The entire day was an exercise in deprivation. He counted the minutes until he would see her. It was exactly the sort of weakness he dreaded in himself, but he finally began to breathe again when he entered his apartment to dress for their dinner with a general and his wife.

That was when he was informed Galila wouldn't be joining them.

"The queen was feeling under the weather and canceled all her engagements for the rest of the week," her assistant informed him.

Shock and concern washed through him in a sickly wave.

"Why wasn't I informed?" He started to brush past her into Galila's rooms.

"She's not here, Your Highness," the woman quickly said. "I thought—it must be my mistake. I understood she intended to speak to you before she left."

Something inside him snapped. Broke. Exploded. "Where the hell did she go?"

The girl fell back a step, eyes wide. "I believe she went to stay with your mother."

* * *

Galila was beating herself up for being the neediest wimp alive, scurrying off for TLC in the desert palace.

She discovered, however, that being needy could be a good thing. Sometimes a person needed someone to coddle and fuss over. Galila's low spirits pulled a maternal instinct from Karim's mother that put a smile of warmth on the older woman's face. A brightness of purpose.

"I'm so glad you came to me. Of course, you should come anytime you feel a need to get away," Tahirah said in response to Galila's apology for imposing. "You'll be a new mother soon. Learn to let people take care of you."

Her spoiling and attention was so sincere, Galila wanted to cry with gratitude. Here was the mother she desperately needed. They talked pregnancy and babies and the challenge of running a palace and the endless social obligations of royal duties.

She was still scorched by Karim's refusal to love her, but at least she had someone who seemed genuinely happy to bond with her. Her heart would still be in two pieces, but at least those pieces could be offered to his mother and the child he gave her. Her life would not be completely devoid of love.

Those broken pieces of her heart jangled when Karim rang through on a video call as she was dressing for dinner. She dismissed her maid and answered.

He looked surprisingly incensed. "What are you doing there?" he snapped.

"I was going to discuss this with you over breakfast this morning, but you weren't there." Completely true, but rather than seek him out or text him or try to inform him via the many other avenues of communication available at the palace, she had slipped away like a criminal. "I'm not here to tell her anything, if that's what you're worried about. I just needed some time."

"For what?"

"To think about how I'm going to accept the kind of marriage you've offered."

"We went over this in the early days, Galila. It will be fine."

"For you. But I fell in love with you. I didn't expect that to happen, but it did. And you don't feel the same. Can't. So I need to think about all of that."

"And do what?" His tone sharpened. "If you think you're going back to Khalia, or taking my child to Europe—"

"If I wanted to do that, I would already be there, wouldn't I? I came to your mother's, Karim. That's as far as I plan on taking your child without your permission. We're having a lovely visit so let me be."

His mouth tightened. "When are you coming back?"

"I haven't decided."

"I'll send the helicopter tomorrow."

"I just got here! Why would you even want me to come back? We're not sleeping together. You barely speak to me. I'm surprised you noticed I was gone."

His nostrils flared as he drew a deep, patience-seeking breath.

"What?" she goaded. "You don't even like when I help with your royal duties. You said so. I make you feel weak. You never needed me before we married and still don't want to, judging by the way you've been treating me. Go back to your old life, then. Pretend I don't exist."

"Galila, if you're trying to provoke some kind of reaction—"

"I know that's impossible! You feel nothing, Karim! We both know you're not going to kill yourself if I stay a few days with your mother so that's exactly what I'm doing."

She jammed the button to end the call.

Then she threw the phone across the room. It hit a marble column, shattering the screen.

"Her Highness has broken her phone," Galila's assistant informed Karim the next morning. "A new one is on its way. She'll be back online this afternoon, I'm sure. In the meanwhile, you'll have to message her through your mother. May

I also ask…? There are a number of agenda items I needed to discuss with her, but in her absence, will you approve these?"

Karim went through them quickly, resenting every second of it. Why? Not because he didn't want to review the preliminary budget for the women's health center. He would have to do that eventually anyway, but because he was staring at an empty chair, speaking instead of listening.

We both know you won't kill yourself…

He forced himself to proceed through his day, thinking of her constantly. He kept making mental notes to share things with her only to realize he wouldn't see her later. He wouldn't watch her painted mouth as she entertained their guests, wouldn't stand with pride beside her, wouldn't set his hand in the middle of her back just so the silken fall of her hair would caress his skin.

By the time he was alone in his library, he was thinking for the first time in his life how good a shot of whiskey might taste.

Furious, he yanked open the curtain and glared at the balcony. Instead of seeing his father there, he saw Galila, tall and strong, chin up, eyes on the horizon.

By your logic, I should drown myself.

Was she hurting? Was that why she had run away? Breaking her heart had never been his intention. Collateral damage was inevitable in life, but he tried not to purposefully hurt anyone. Galila, with her spirit and compassion and sharp intelligence, deserved every speck of the adoration she earned.

She had definitely earned his respect, not only solving the mystery of her mother's lover, but protecting that secret as diligently as he always had. She had been reluctant to tell *him*, and he knew how heavy the load was on that.

It was considerably lighter these days, he realized. Because he had shared it with her? Or because he was carrying a different load on his conscience? Her bruised heart crushed like a piano atop his own.

He turned to stare at the lion on the bookshelf, the one engraved with the words *Where Is She?*

The same question clawed inside him. His mate

was in a palace in the desert. She might as well
be locked in a vault the way the lioness was.
Locked in the dark for safekeeping. Endlessly
searching for her mate while this one eternally
waited here.

Apart.

Why? Why did it have to be this way?

With a snarl, he grabbed the bookend, tempted
to throw it through the glass doors and over the
balcony, into the sea.

Instead, he carried it with him to his empty
bedroom.

Galila was treading water in the infinity pool that
overlooked the oasis when she heard her maid
make a startled noise. She dragged her gaze from
the sand dunes and palms, swirling in the water
to face the paved courtyard that surrounded the
pool.

Her husband picked up her robe off the chair
while her maid scampered away.

Her chin was in the water and Galila very
nearly sucked a mouthful into her lungs, man-

aging at the last second to merely swallow a taste of chlorine.

"Come," Karim said, shaking out her robe. "I want to talk."

She hesitated, then kicked herself into a glide toward the steps, self-conscious as she climbed them. Her body hadn't changed. She was barely pregnant, but she didn't know which would be worse—his avid gaze or a disinterested one.

He gave her a rapacious one. His features hardened as his attention followed the flow of water off her shoulders, between her breasts and across her quivering belly, over the triangle of green-blue bikini bottoms and down her thighs and calves.

Shaken, she couldn't find a voice to ask what he was doing there. She turned to thread her arms into the sleeves of the robe, then caught the edges and folded them across her front. The silk clung to her wet skin, warm despite being in the shade.

He didn't let her step away. His arms closed around her and held her before him, damp hair under his chin. He trapped her arms in a criss-cross before she could get the belt tied.

"Karim—"

"Shh," he commanded softly. "Let me feel you. I need to know that you are here."

"You knew exactly where I was." She didn't know why, but her heart began to pepper even harder in her chest. Her body twitched with un-certainty. Relax? Remain on guard? "Why are *you* here, Karim?"

"To tell you that we don't have to repeat his-tory. We shouldn't."

"In what way? Because you've already made it clear you won't allow yourself to feel anything toward me," she said with a jagged edge on her voice. Most especially not the depth of love his father had felt for her mother.

His arms tightened and his beard brushed her wet cheek as he spoke against her skin. "I don't know that I had a choice in how I feel about you. From the moment I saw you, I was transfixed."

Her insides juddered in reaction while she recalled that luminescent moment of turning to see him watching her.

"So was I," she whispered in stark honesty.

"The difference is, you were willing to accept how I made you feel. I was never going to allow myself to be this vulnerable, Galila. I knew I couldn't afford it. I had to fight it."

"Because you don't trust me." She pushed out of his arms and turned to confront him.

"Be careful," he said through gritted teeth, glancing toward an upper balcony to indicate they could be overheard by his mother at any moment.

"I know," she hissed. "But that secret is the reason you married me, yet you withheld it from me. Even when things changed. At least, I thought things were changing." She touched where her heart was a cracked and brittle thing in her chest. "You made me think we were growing close, that we could trust one another, but no. You were keeping secrets, refusing to care..." Her voice trailed into a whisper. The despair that had been stalking her crept close enough to swallow her whole.

"Galila." He tried to reach for her.

She held him off with an upraised hand, too raw to accept his touch without crying under the agony of a caress that wasn't genuine tenderness or affection.

He flinched at her rejection.

"I trust you," he said gravely. "If I didn't, I wouldn't have let you stay here like this. I know you'll guard what you know as carefully as I do. I wouldn't be having a child with you if I didn't trust you."

"But you don't trust me with your heart! What do you think I'm going to do with it? Treat it as badly as you treat mine?"

He snapped his head back, breath hissing in with shock, as though she had struck far deeper than he had imagined anyone could.

There was no satisfaction in it. It made her feel small. She looked to the arid sands of the desert, a perfect reflection of their future.

"I'm not trying to hurt you," she murmured.

"I'm just not ready to be with you and act like I'm happy when I'm not."

"You won't be until you come back to me, Galila. We have to be together."

She started to shake her head, but he spoke with more insistence.

"The denial is what does the damage. Pushing you away is killing me." His tone was an odd mix of vehemence and tenderness.

She glanced at him, not wanting the unfurling of hope again, only to open herself for a stomping.

"You were right," he continued. "I won't kill myself over your absence."

And there it was. Her heart went into free fall toward a shattering impact.

"I will come after you and fight to keep you. I *am* fighting for you." His possessive words, the light of anguished need in his expression, was a hand that thrust out and caught her heart before it hit the ground, dragging it into his possession so it would be his forever. *"Come home."*

Her mouth trembled. "I want to, but—"

"I love you, Galila."

Her knees weakened.

He caught her with real hands this time, grasping her upper arms and holding her in front of him so all she saw was him. His features were hard, but cast in angles of concern and repentance. His eyes gleamed dark and solemn, but they were open windows to his soul, holding back none of the brilliant light within him. A light that shone with ardent, aching love as he scanned her features.

It was such a startling, intimate look into his own heart, hot tears of emotion brimmed in her eyes and a lump formed in her throat.

The rest of her crumbled. Not in a bad way. In the best possible way, even though she was quite sure it was her least elegant look ever. Her chin crinkled and she had to bite her lips while tears of joy and love overflowed her eyes. Her face was clean of makeup, her hair skimmed flat, her robe damp and ruffled as she hugged herself into him. Hard.

"I love you, too," she choked. "So much."

She lifted her mouth and he brought his head down. Their lips met in a kiss that made her cry out at the power of it. The sweet perfection. He kissed her the way he had that first night in the garden outside the palace of Khalia. Like he was released from years of restraint.

She returned his passion with her own overwhelming need for him, ignoring the aching tenderness in her breasts in favor of pressing closer and closer—

"Karim!" his mother called sharply from an upper terrace. "*The servants.* Take that to your room."

He pulled away from their kiss as they both broke into laughter.

CHAPTER TEN

KARIM WOKE DISORIENTED in the darkness of a tent. He was quickly distracted by his wife's exploring touch over his body. She was staking a claim here in the dark, taking her time, teasing him with the swish of her hair across his skin, kissing and arousing him.

His hands sought her breasts and he remembered at the last moment to be extra gentle, letting her press into his touch as much as she could bear.

"I thought you were too tired for this," he whispered in the dark, longing to suck on her nipples, but he could only tongue them or she cried, they were so sensitive.

"I was." She sighed. "Then I woke up and I didn't want to sleep. *I want you.*"

She straddled him so he felt her nest against his

shaft. It had been a long day of travel finding this particular tribe. They'd been welcomed warmly and given the royal treatment, but Galila was in a delicate condition and had turned in early.

She was proving very resilient now, though. He held himself in position as he felt her seeking to take him inside her heat.

They both sighed as she seated herself on him, her heat snug around his pulsing shaft. She began an undulation that made him bite back a groan of supreme pleasure. They didn't have wind and the pepper of whipped sand to disguise their carnal noises this time.

Catching back her own moans of pleasure, she gave herself to him without reserve. He did the same, lifting his hips to meet the return of hers. Her fingernails dug into his chest where she braced herself and hit her peak quickly, the power of it so acute, she pulled him over with her.

He was sorry for it to be over so quickly, but they were practically in public. It was close to dawn and the arrival of other royal guests could happen any time. Today, tomorrow. It might be in a few days, they had been told, but eventually Adir would show up with his wife.

As their personal storm receded, Galila lay sleepily upon him, still joined with him. Her lips grazed his damp skin as she spoke.

"What do you think he will say?"

"I don't know," he said truthfully. That was what he was here to find out.

Galila was watching a new mother demonstrate the proper way to swaddle an infant when excited voices drew her attention to the arriving party.

"Amira!" She leaped to her feet with excitement. Her friend was considerably further along than she was, showing well into her second trimester.

Amira hugged her warmly, but it was the beaming smile on her face that put Galila most at ease. She hadn't seen Adir since the shocking morning of Zufar's wedding. He still had the dangerous air about him and watched her closely as she reunited with Amira, but when he gazed on his wife, he revealed a glimpse of tenderness that warmed Galila's heart.

That softness disappeared between one blink and the next as he flicked his gaze from her to Karim. His stance shifted imperceptibly, almost as if he felt Karim was an enemy he had to watch for sudden moves.

Karim wore the same air of armed caution, unabashed in the way he took Adir's measure.

"Meet my husband," Galila invited Amira, stepping back to Karim's side as she made the introductions.

The resemblance between Karim and Adir wasn't obvious, but she was looking for it and saw the way Karim noted their similar height and scanned a brow and a jaw that matched his own. Seeing their profiles reflected like that, the similarity was undeniable to her. Strange and endearing, especially because she saw a hint of her brothers in Adir as well.

"What business do you have with me?" Adir asked Karim.

"My wife wanted to see her friend, to assure herself she was well." He nodded at Amira.

"Very," Adir said flatly. "As you can see."

Amira patted her baby bump. "All three of us are very happy."

"I'm glad," Galila said. "But we also wanted to speak with you, Adir. About…" She looked to Karim. This was such a delicate matter. "It's a private matter. We have something for you. But I think…" She looked between Adir and Amira, able to see the obvious connection between husband and wife. "Amira, you should come, too."

They entered the tent that Galila and Karim occupied. Amira accompanied them, a confused look on her face. Galila gave her hand a small squeeze and offered a smile of reassurance as she lowered to the cushions with her.

Adir waited while Karim brought the parcel they'd carried into the desert with them, then sat as Karim did.

The bookends were both wrapped carefully in linen. Galila helped Karim unravel them until the lion and lioness were both revealed.

Karim set the lion on the mat before Adir. Then he took the heavy lioness from Galila and braced the two upright walls back to back.

Now it looked as though the male lion gazed on his mate with a casual check-in. *Stay close, sweetheart.* She peered over at him. *I'm right here, darling.*

"A wedding gift?" Adir said, voice somewhere between dry sarcasm and suspicion. But it was clear he saw the value in the pieces and found it odd they were offering such a treasure to him.

Galila licked her lips. "This one belonged to my mother."

Karim's cheeks went hollow before he nodded at the lion. "The other was my father's. We think you should have them."

Adir's brows slammed together.

Amira gasped. "Are you saying…?"

Karim nodded once, curt. He was wary, she could tell, because she knew her husband well these days. She wanted to take his hand, but there were still times where he needed his walls. This was one of them.

Adir looked between them, astonished. He picked up both pieces and turned them over.

"There's nothing to prove it," Karim said. "Except that I know it to be true."

"That your father is—"

"Was. He passed away when I was six. A few months before you were born."

Adir drew a harsh breath. "You're saying we're brothers?" He was clearly astounded, but studied Karim with more interest.

Karim was doing the same to him. "I didn't know there was a child. Not until the night of Zufar's wedding, when Galila told me."

"These are so beautiful," Amira murmured, taking up the lioness.

"Are you sure you want to give them up?" Adir looked between them.

"It's best if questions aren't asked in my palace about how we found the mate," Karim said. "And it seems right that you should have something of them."

Adir nodded and set aside the lion, thoughtful. "Volatile information, indeed. Thank you for entrusting me with it." He shot a look at Galila and the corner of his mouth quirked. "Good thing I never intend to talk about this, since I would have to tell people that my brother and sister are married."

She gave his knee a nudge. "Exactly the sort of misplaced remark I expect from a brother."

His mouth quirked and he looked to Karim again. "I've always wondered who my father might be. What was he like?"

"That was a wonderful trip, but it's good to be home," Galila said as they entered their apartment. The doors between their rooms were rarely closed these days.

"What are you most excited for? A proper bath? Or Wi-Fi?"

"Privacy with my husband," she said, pinching at his stomach as she walked past him toward the bathroom. "Join me in the bath?"

"Love to. I'll be in as soon as I check—" He cut himself off with a sharp curse.

Galila swung back, instantly concerned. "What's wrong?"

"I don't know if it's *wrong*, but your brother has abdicated."

"Zufar? *Why?*"

"To rule Rumadah, Niesha's home country."

"What?" Her ears rang under the news. "Then who is king of Khalia?"

His head came up. "Your brother Malak."

She blinked in shock. "God help us all."

* * * * *